Penny

PENNY

Story and pictures by
MARJORIE
TORREY

HOWELL, SOSKIN, PUBLISHERS

To
Annie

Penny

1. THE MAN IN THE TRAIN

PENNY SAT UP stiffly on the green plush seat. Beside her was her valise and her little umbrella; also Rosmyrelda, her favorite doll, and a box of lunch, and a story-book to read if she "got tired of looking out of the windows," Mother had said. But Penny was sure she would never grow tired of riding on a train. It was too exciting. She remembered how the distant whistles sounded in the night, when the trains sped past, going to strange faraway places, wonderful places that she would think about as she fell asleep again. And now, she would see them. She was going on a journey.

She wanted it to begin.

She wished the train would start. But she was worried that when it did Father might not have time to get off. Yet she did not like to tell him to go. That would not seem very polite.

"Well, Pusskin, I hope you and Aunt Penelope will have a fine time together," Father said. "And you'll write and tell Mother and me all about it, won't you?" Penny nodded.

"And you won't forget, or fall asleep and ride past your station, will you? Remember, it's East Riverbridge."

"Of course I'll remember, Father," Penny said.

"All abo-o-oard!" shouted the conductor.

"Hurry, Father—the train's going to start!" urged Penny.

But Father did not seem to be worried about that. "Open your fist—and shut your eyes!" he said.

Excited little shivers were going up her back, but Penny did as she was told and felt something smooth and round and flat slipped into her palm under her glove, and her fingers folded over it. Then she opened her eyes, and Father kissed her.

"Have a good time, darling. And come back all fine and fat and rosy!" he said.

Then there was a jerk, and the wheels ground, and the train began to move, and Father went swinging up the aisle. At the door he stopped for a moment to speak to the conductor, who looked back at Penny and nodded and smiled. Penny knew that he had been told to "keep an eye" on her, and not let her ride past East Riverbridge; and she felt a little offended. After all, even if she *was* small for her age she was eight-going-on-nearly-nine, and *she* knew she was very grown-up in her mind.

But Penny did not have much time to think about that, because she was pressing her nose against the window watching for Father. Ah, there he was, coming back along the platform, looking up and waving. She waved back, and he walked along beside the train as it moved, smiling and saying something she could not hear. She threw him a kiss, and he caught it and put it on his lips and smacked them, and formed the word "Delicious!" Then the train was moving so fast that he could not keep up with it any longer. . . .

Penny settled back in her seat. She straightened Rosmyrelda, who had fallen forward on her china nose. Then she slowly opened her left hand and unbuttoned her glove. Father had given her a whole, bright new silver dollar!

She felt very grown-up indeed as she opened the little red-leather purse that hung from her wrist by a silver chain and put the big dollar into it, together with a dime and a nickel and six pennies that she had saved herself, from her allowance. Her ticket was there, too; and a tiny slab of chocolate wrapped in tin-foil, from the slot-machine on the station platform. This she would not touch until after she had eaten her lunch, she decided. She snapped her purse shut and folded her hands, and turned to watch the houses and streets whizzing past the window.

Suddenly the train went into a tunnel. The car was as dark as if it were night time, and away up ahead, where the engine was, the whistle blew. Whoo—*oo*-OOOO! it went, with a hollow sound, like the loud, echoing noise it made when you shouted in the curved tunnel under the bridge in Central Park. And the wheels were making a great clatter—clackety-CLACK-clack, clackety-clack-CLACK, CLACK-ETY-clack-clack. Then out they came again into the sunshine. Rosmyrelda looked quite startled, Penny thought.

After that they flashed through several shorter tunnels. And after that the houses were smaller and farther apart, until, sometimes, there were none at all. Then there would be just one, with meadows around it, and perhaps cows, and trees; and hills looking very blue in the distance—bluer than the sky. Then there would be more houses again, and the train would blow its whistle shrilly, and soon would slow up, and stop at a station.

Now and then there were houses with yards close up to the railroad tracks, and in one of these hollyhocks grew all along the fence, and half-a-dozen children were playing, running after each other, laughing and shouting. Their clothes were dirty and they were barefoot; Penny thought they seemed to be having marvelous fun. She wondered if Aunt Penelope would let her go barefoot. Surely she would! For after all she lived in the country, and children often went barefoot in the country. Penny knew that from picture books and stories—and now she had seen them!

She began to wonder about her aunt—or rather her great-aunt; Aunt Penelope was really Father's auntie. What would she be like? Although Aunt Penelope had come to visit them once in New York, Penny had been a very little baby then and could not remember anything about it. But surely Aunt Penelope must be nice or Penny would not have been named after her. . . .

Yes, she must be *very* nice, thought the little girl; probably something like Father, with a gay twinkle in her eyes and a loving smile. She would live in a snug little white house, with bright-painted shutters on the outside and crisp muslin curtains on the inside of the small, latticed windows. There would be a big red barn, and horses and cows and little calves, and of course fluffy chicks, and baby pigs, and lambs frolicking, kicking up their tiny hooves. And all around there would be fields full of buttercups and daisies, and nearby, a brook where cat-tails grew and wild lilies—and maybe even watercress! She did hope there would be watercress, for ever since she had read a book called "Sunshine and Shadow in Katherine's Life" she had wanted to pick watercress, all fresh and green, from the edge of a bubbling stream running through a sunshiny meadow.

Penny sighed and moved restlessly. She wished the train would hurry; it seemed that she had been on it for a long while. She wondered what time it was. Certainly it must be time now to eat her lunch. Anyway, she was hungry. And it would be fun to see what Mother had packed in the box, wrapped in shiny paper and tied with a red-and-silver string.

She unknotted the string carefully and put it away in the pocket of her blue reefer jacket, to keep. And she folded the paper and laid it on the seat beside her, because her mother said only inconsiderate people threw crumpled messy paper from picnic boxes around. Then she opened the cardboard box.

There were two sandwiches in it, cut crossways—which really made four, two of chicken and two spread with peach jam. These were wrapped in paper napkins and beneath them nestled a tangerine and an apple and three ginger cookies shaped like stars.

Penny ate the sandwiches first, then she peeled the tangerine, putting the peel in the box. She quartered the fruit and ate each small section slowly, for tangerines were a treat; besides she wanted to make it all last as long as she could.

When she came to the cookies and picked up the first one she had a sharp memory of her mother's pretty hands with their round pink nails and the three rings she always wore, cutting the dough into different shapes—crescents, diamonds, three-leaved clovers and stars. Penny liked the star-shaped ones the best, and Mother had remembered that . . .

What would Mother be doing now? All at once she seemed very, very far away, and Penny wanted to see her very, very much.

But of course she couldn't. She wouldn't see her for a long, long time . . .

This thought gave her a peculiarly empty feeling in her stomach, yet she was not hungry any more. She didn't want to eat her apple now; she put it away in her satchel. She didn't even want to eat the little bar of chocolate that she had been looking forward to. And the last bite of cookie stuck in her throat as it went down.

She brushed the crumbs from her lap and sat up straighter. When *would* the train reach East Riverbridge? Surely they must be nearly there; they had been traveling for hours and hours and hours. And nothing very interesting was to be seen now from the windows—just more fields and trees sliding by, and now and then another lonely house in the distance. And the sun slanted in, getting in her eyes. Either that, or something else, made them blink and water, so that she had to rub them hard with her knuckles.

Just then a voice said, *"Hurrumph.* Feeling homesick, little girl?"

Penny looked up. An old man sitting across the aisle leaned toward her, putting down the book he had been reading.

"Don't cry," he said. "Come over here and I'll tell you a nice story—all about Goldilocks and the three bears." He patted the seat beside him.

Penny felt her face getting hot, from her neck right up to her forehead. "Why, he thinks I'm a *baby!*" she thought. "Well, I s-suppose I do look as if I'm crying, and—and maybe I am so it serves me right."

But that didn't make her feel any better. In fact it made her cross at herself and cross at the old man too. Why did he have to *notice?* she thought, and turned away to stare out of the window again without answering.

She sat there stiff as a poker, more and more miserable because she had been rude, which made the empty unhappy feeling inside her even worse. But what could she do now? She didn't know what to say to the old gentleman; she didn't want to say anything. She wasn't sure, either, what kind of sound her voice might make when it came out, her throat felt so tight and uncomfortable. But she had to try, to be polite, so she turned slowly and looked across the aisle.

But the old man was reading again and did not glance up from his book.

Penny stared out of the window until finally her neck began to ache. She leaned her head back, but when she did that the back of the seat made her sailor hat push forward over her nose. She thought, "It must look silly . . . well, I don't care if it does, it keeps the sun out of my eyes, and besides I'm tired of these same, same fields always going by . . . I'm awfully, awfully tired . . . "

She sighed, and reached out her arm for Rosmyrelda . . . and closed her eyes . . .

2. LUMP IN YOUR THROAT

"WAKE UP, little girl!" Penny felt her shoulder being gently shaken. She opened her eyes and sat up, pushing back her hat, to see the Conductor bending over her. "We're coming into East Riverbridge," he said.

He picked up her valise. Penny clutched Rosmyrelda and her story book and her umbrella, slid off the green plush seat and followed him down the aisle. Her knees were a little wobbly. She must have slept quite a long while, because the lamps in the car were lighted now, and outside the windows it was almost dark.

By the time they reached the door the train had stopped. The conductor went down the steps and set down her valise, then he reached up to swing her to the platform. But Penny drew back. She still felt abashed at having gone to sleep; she did not want to be carried. Holding to the cold black iron railing she climbed down the steep steps by herself.

"Hmm. Proud little piece, ain't you?" said the Conductor. But his voice was kind and he was smiling. "I've got one at home just like you, a little granddaughter." He peered along the Depot platform. "Well, here's your Auntie. Goodbye, missy!"

He waved his lantern, then swung himself up the steps and the train jerked and began to move.

"Goodbye!" called Penny. The Conductor waved to her, and the whistle went *Whooo-ooo-ooo!* The long line of lighted windows twinkled past. The train looked cosy and mysterious now, as it sped away.

As Penny stared after it, she wished, suddenly, that it was going in the other direction and that she was on it, flying back home. How beautiful Mother had looked in her peppermint-striped dress with the puffed sleeves, waving goodbye from the high stoop as Penny and Father jumped into the hansom cab to ride off to the train. At the time Penny had been too excited to think of it but now she remembered how especially bright and held-wide-open her mother's eyes had been; she wondered, was Mother trying not to cry? and her own eyes smarted as she looked up at the old lady coming toward her.

Could this really be Aunt Penélope? How very, very old she was! And how oddly she stared at Penny. She stared so long, without saying anything and without even smiling, that Penny began to wonder if her face were dirty. Or—perhaps this strange old lady was deciding that she did not like her.

Yes, that must be it, thought Penny.

"I suppose she expected me to be pretty, with pink cheeks and curly hair. Well, I can't help it if my nose turns up and my hair doesn't—and besides, some people do make me *feel* pretty—Father does!"

She gazed back at her aunt.

At last the old lady cleared her throat and said, "How do you do, Penny," and held out a hand in a tight black kid glove.

It took Penny a moment to change Rosmyrelda and the story-book to her left arm and give her Aunt the right hand properly.

"How-do-you-do, Aunt Penelope. I am very well, thank you," she said.

They shook hands, stiffly. Then an old colored man who had been standing a short distance away came forward and Aunt Penelope said, "This is Jonah. Jonah, this is my niece, Miss Penny."

"How-do-you-do, Mister Jonah," said Penny.

"How-do, Miss," said the old man, touching his hat. He picked up Penny's valise, and she and Aunt Penelope followed him around the depot, where a beautiful brown sleek horse was tied to a post; behind him was a two-seated carriage with a fringed canopy over it.

Jonah started to help Aunt Penelope into the back seat, but she waved him away. She climbed slowly in and sat down.

"Come, child," she said.

Penny climbed in beside her, old Jonah took his place behind the brown horse and they started off.

Then Penny saw a long pointed black nose and two shiny black eyes watching her from the seat beside Jonah. She leaned forward eagerly and saw that the eyes were shaded by a black fringe tied up with a red ribbon. Beneath that there was a great puff of frizzy black hair like a muff, and a small body covered with curly fur that looked like Mother's astrakhan cape.

Penny said, "Is—is that your dog, Aunt Penelope?"

"Yes. He is a French poodle. His name is Pouf," said Aunt Penelope. "You need not be afraid of him, he is a very well-behaved dog."

Penny had never had a dog of her own, because Mother said the city was no place for them. But she had always wanted one and she had petted neighbor dogs and even stray dogs. She had never thought of being afraid of them. She leaned forward now to pet Pouf.

But he drew away, looking very dignified, and turned around to sit haughtily beside Jonah as they rode onward. Penny took her hand back and clasped it tightly around Rosmyrelda.

She didn't say anything after that, nor did Aunt Penelope.

After a long drive they came to a large scrolled-iron gate set in a tall spiked iron fence. Jonah climbed out of the carriage and opened the gate. Then he drove in, got down again and closed the gate, and resumed his perch. The wheels crunched on a wide winding graveled road as they drove toward a large tall house surrounded by trees.

"Welcome to The Elms," said Aunt Penelope.

Penny thought of the forest around the castle of the Sleeping Beauty. The house, in the twilight, did look like a castle, silhouetted against the green-and-gold colored sky.

But inside it did not seem at all like a castle. Mister Jonah led them through a hall into a long room. He turned up a kerosene lamp under a round frosted globe, and went away, with Penny's valise.

Aunt Penelope took off her bonnet and cloak, and said, "Did you have a nice journey?"

"Yes, thank you," said Penny.

"Well, tea will be ready soon. Meanwhile, I will show you your room. It—it used to be your Father's room. I hope you will like it. And you will want to wash your hands and tidy your hair," said Aunt Penelope.

She went ahead and Penny followed up a curving stairway, and then along a dimly lit hall to a small room in which there was a narrow high bed with a little ladder leading up to it and a canopy above it. Penny's valise was on a chair. She put Rosmyrelda and her book beside it, and took off her hat and her reefer jacket.

Aunt Penelope showed her to the bathroom at the end of the hall, and waited outside while she washed her face and hands and combed her hair. Then they went downstairs.

Mister Jonah was waiting in the hall. He said, "Tea is ready, Miss Penelope," and led the way into a large room with a long table in the center of it. He held Aunt Penelope's high-backed chair, which was at one end of the long table; then he held Penny's, which was away off at the other end. In between them were two tall silver candelabra holding lighted candles, and because of these, and the length of the table, and the fact that Penny's face did not come very far above it, she could hardly see her Aunt. And she did not see any food at all, except some fruit in an alabaster bowl in the exact middle of the white tablecloth.

Mister Jonah went silently out of a swinging door covered with green felt, with a small oval glass window in it. He came back with a large platter, on which was some cold ham, sliced very thin. This he passed first to Aunt Penelope, then to Penny. Afterwards he brought biscuits, lemon jelly and sponge cake, and tea for Aunt Penelope and milk for Penny.

The big dining room was rather chilly and shadowy in the corners and very quiet. Aunt Penelope did not speak, except once to ask if Penny would like another piece of cake or some more lemon jelly.

Penny said, "No, thank you."

She could not swallow very well, because there was a lump in her throat. She was thinking of the round table with the cheerful big lamp in the center, in the basement dining room at home, and Mother and Father and herself talking and laughing together as they ate supper. And of the big dictionary with the cushion on it, in her own special chair. And of the cosy smell of toast—golden brown, hot buttery toast that she often helped to make, holding it on a long fork over the coals in the kitchen stove. The lump in her throat swelled. She could not finish her slice of cake, though she tried for politeness' sake. But perhaps her Aunt would not notice, far away there at the other end of the table. She certainly did not seem to be paying any attention. She sipped her tea slowly, and took small slow bites of food.

At last the meal was over and they went back into the long parlor with the frosted lamp. Aunt Penelope sat at one side of the coal fire in the small grate and Penelope sat opposite her, in a high-backed chair covered with black horse-hair that scratched her legs even through her ribbed stockings. Pouf the poodle dog was sitting on the hearth-rug, and Penny longed to curl up beside him with her arm around him. If she could do that—if she could just be close to someone, she thought—the lump in her throat might go away. But the poodle sat gazing into the fire without turning his head, and Penny remembered that he had been very haughty toward her when she had first wanted to make friends with him. So she just sat in her stiff high-backed chair, looking at the neat red ribbon bow that tied up Pouf's thick kinky bangs and trying not to let the tears creep out from underneath her eyelids.

Tick-tock, tick-tock, tick-tock, said the tall clock in a dim corner of the room. But how slowly it went! At this rate it would be a million years before her visit to Aunt Penelope was over and she could go home to Mother and Father.

Tick-tock, tick-tock, tick-tock . . .

Finally Aunt Penelope looked up over the afghan she was crocheting and said, "When is your bedtime, Penny?"

"Nine o'clock, Aunt Penelope," answered Penny.

The hands of the clock pointed to sixteen minutes past eight.

Aunt Penelope cleared her throat and said, "Would you like to look at my album? It is there on the center table. And there is a story-book, too. It was your father's, when he was a boy."

Penny got the story-book from the round table covered with a crimson lambriquin, under the lamp. It was called Moby Dick, and she expected it would be very interesting because it had been her father's. But she couldn't understand what it was all about, and after a while she put it down and opened the big album.

She turned the pages slowly, pausing when she came to the picture of a little boy or girl or a baby The photographs were old and faded and the children wore quaint old-fashioned clothes. Penny wondered who they were. She wanted to ask, but when she glanced up she saw that her Aunt had put down her crocheting and was reading the newspaper. Penny did not like to interrupt. She sighed, and closed the album.

Tick-tock, tick-tock, tick-tock, droned the clock.

But at last, at last it struck the hour—nine times.

Aunt Penelope put down her newspaper. She looked at Penny, who was sitting with her hands clasped tightly in her lap and staring into the fire.

The old lady said, "There is a night-lamp burning in your bedroom, my dear. Shall I—would you like me to come upstairs, to help you undress—or—or anything?"

Her voice sounded stiff. And so did Penny's as she replied, "I can undress myself, Aunt. Thank you."

"Well—I'll come up when you're in bed, and say good-night," said her Aunt, taking up her crocheting again.

Penny went upstairs, through the shadowy hall dimly

lighted by one gas-jet in the big brass chandelier. After she had undressed and brushed her teeth and said her prayers she climbed into the high bed. She took Rosmyrelda in her arms and held her closely. Then, as she heard her Aunt's footsteps slowly climbing the stairs, she pushed the doll further under the covers.

"She'd think it babyish to take a doll to bed, I guess," thought the little girl. "Aunt doesn't know I've had Rosmyrelda as long as I can remember and before that she was Mother's and she's really more like an intimate friend than a doll—"

Her Aunt came into the room. "Well, you got to bed quickly," she said. She hesitated, then asked, "Shall I hear you say your prayers?"

"I've said them, Aunt—thank you," answered Penny.

"Then—I'll just open the window," said her Aunt. When she had done so she asked if Penny wanted the night-light left burning?

Penny did, but somehow she didn't like to say so. She shook her head.

"I'll leave it in the hall, anyway," said Aunt Penelope. She picked up the little lamp, then paused beside the bed. "Goodnight, my dear," she said.

"Goodnight, Aunt Penelope," said Penny.

Her Aunt stood there a moment. Then she stooped and her cool old lips touched Penny's forehead.

"I'll leave your door ajar. My room is just across the hall, if you want anything, my dear," she said.

When she had gone Penny lay there under the thick quilts feeling very small and alone. The big house was so still, yet every now and then it *creaked;* and from the dark lonely night outside came the mournful drone of katydids, and the hoarse croaking of frogs. She longed for the cheerful street noises she was used to; for the sound of Father's voice as he read aloud or talked with Mother in a nearby room; for her Mother's goodnight hug and kiss.

"I suppose I *am* babyish, Rosmyrelda. Only I didn't know it would be like this," she whispered, drawing the doll closer. But the china head was hard and cold against her cheek. "And I don't feel sleepy—and the night will never, never end."

Just at that moment she heard an odd, pattering sound —quick, very light footsteps, padding across the floor. And then a small weight landed on the bed, on her feet. She sat up, and by the dim light that came through the half-opened door she saw Pouf, the poodle.

Penny reached her hand out and gently touched his thick mane. He crept nearer and laid his soft moist nose on her shoulder. She put her arm around him, feeling comforted; and after a while she fell asleep.

3.   A BIG, STILL HOUSE

WHEN PENNY WOKE UP the sun was streaming across her pillow.

At first, still half asleep, she did not know why she was in a strange room. She thought she was having a dream—for sometimes Penny's dreams were very vivid indeed. She stared up at the white canopy of dotted muslin above the bed, and at the unfamiliar wall paper, striped and with a pattern that slightly resembled large beetles—not at all like that of her own little room, which was covered with tiny butterflies and rosebuds; at the clock on the mantel with its hands pointing to ten minutes past seven, and at Rosmyrelda beside her. Then she remembered where she was, and looked for Pouf. But the little dog was gone.

Still, he *had* been there with her, he had come into her room and jumped onto the bed and cuddled up in her arms.

"He *does* like me!" thought Penny. It was a comforting thought; and it was rather fun to climb down the steps from the funny high bed. The sun was warm and bright, too, and she felt quite cheerful as she washed and dressed herself quickly. She put on a green gingham frock and a white pinafore and hurried downstairs, taking Rosmyrelda with her. Perhaps Aunt Penelope would not be so silent and stiff as she had seemed last night. And she hoped Pouf would come running to greet her.

But he did not. Nor did anyone else. In fact there seemed no one astir in the big house.

"Perhaps it is too early and they're still asleep," thought Penny.

But her heart sank a little, and her footsteps sounded loud in the hall, which was large and cold and dim, with only two narrow strips of light coming through the frosted patterned glass on either side of the carved mahogany door. Penny stopped, and looked around. A huge stag's head with enormous branching antlers seemed to stare at her, its

large glassy eyes mournful and forbidding. "What are *you* doing here, little girl?" it seemed to be thinking.

But of course it did not speak. Nor was there any sound at all, that Penny could hear.

She tiptoed across the black-and-white marble squares of the floor and parted the heavy velvet drapes at the parlor doorway and peered in. The curtains were still drawn across the high narrow windows, the fire was out, and the room seemed even more solemn than it had the night before. There was no one there.

The dining room, too, was dark and empty. But as Penny stood there in the doorway, she did hear voices. They seemed to come from beyond the green felt door with the little glass window in it.

She waited, hoping someone would appear. No one did. Penny walked slowly across the long room. She hesitated at the door; it was not her own home and she did not like to intrude. But she had guessed, of course, that the kitchen was beyond; she hoped it would be all right for her to go in. She pushed open the swinging door.

She found herself in a pantry, with a sink on one side and cupboards on the other. At the end was a door which, she supposed, must lead to the kitchen. She opened it. As she did so she saw Aunt Penelope, wearing an apron and bending over the stove. Mister Jonah stood beside her, a large tea cloth tied around him. They both turned quickly as Penny came in.

Her aunt's face was flushed. She said, "I didn't know you would be awake so early!" Her voice sounded sharp; Penny thought she seemed annoyed. She added, "Go back into the dining room and sit down. Breakfast will be ready soon."

The big kitchen was warm and bright. Sunshine came in at the windows that had red-and-white-checked curtains at them; rosy coals glowed through openings in the polished black iron range, before which Pouf the poodle sat on a round rag rug. A delicious smell of something baking filled the air, making Penny's small tip-tilted nose crinkle. She longed to stay near the stove in the pleasant cosy room.

But her Aunt had told her to go away, so she obeyed. She hoped Pouf would follow her. He didn't, and as she climbed into her chair in the gloomy dining-room she felt the lump coming back into her throat.

It seemed a long time that she sat there, but finally Aunt Penelope came in followed by Pouf, and went to her place at the other end of the long table. She had taken off the apron and looked stiff and dignified. Soon after she seated herself Mister Jonah came in. He drew the curtains from the windows.

He said, "Good morning, Missy," (as if he had not seen her at all until then) and bowed gravely.

"Good morning, Mister Jonah," Penny replied politely.

He went out and returned with the breakfast.

But the biscuits did not taste as lovely as they had smelled, probably because of the lump in her throat. She could not eat very much and she was glad when the meal was over.

After that they went into the parlor. But although the curtains were drawn aside and the sun slanted between them, it could not get very far into the large room, which was still chilly.

Aunt Penelope sat down, hesitated, then took up her newspaper. Pouf placed himself beside her.

Penny did not know what to do. At home she would have been busy with so many things—there were always more things to do than there was time for! There was her paint-box of water-colors and her Prang's book of outlined pictures to fill in with gay tints; or she might draw her own pictures on her sketch-block with her crayons. Or she could cut paper-dolls from the old magazines her Mother kept especially for her. Or she could sew for Rosmyrelda; or watch her mother in the kitchen, perhaps helping to make cookies and cakes—and scraping the cake-bowl! She might play with Emma and Alice, two little girls who lived down the block. Or she might read—she loved to read.

Well, she could do that now. She went upstairs, got her story-book, and brought it down to the parlor. She sat down with it near Aunt Penelope.

But somehow the pages did not carry her imagination away to interesting places and make her see lovely new people and things, as usually happened when she opened a story-book. Her mind floated away from the printed words. Instead, it kept remembering the bright living room in her home, with the daffodil-patterned walls, and the pretty white-and-gilt-framed pictures, the yellow silk scarves on the table and on the small golden-oak piano. It was a gold-colored, sunny, happy room. And outside in the street people passed. She could swing on the iron gate of the little front yard and watch, and imagine stories about them—the Italian women with their dark faces and gold ear-rings, balancing huge bundles of bread on their stately heads; the ole-clo' man with the bells strung across his wagon; the hucksters of strawberries or bananas, or more beautiful still, of potted hyacinth and geranium. And in the late afternoon, usually at dusk, there would be the hurdy-gurdy . . . .

Penny put down her book.

"Even if I could read it," she thought, "I couldn't go on and on just reading and reading and reading . . . " The clock ticked, tocked, ticked, tocked, ticked, tocked. "I couldn't go on like this for hours and hours—and even days and days—and—and even weeks and weeks. I *couldn't!*"

She got up and went to the window and stood staring out. But there was nothing to see except trees, and grass with an iron deer in the middle of it and a tall iron railing around it. Still, the sun was shining; it certainly looked nicer outside than it did indoors.

"May I go out, Aunt Penelope?" she asked.

"Why yes," said her Aunt. "But of course you won't go outside our gate to play, will you?"

"No, Aunt Penelope," answered Penny. With Rosmyrelda under her arm she walked slowly toward the door. She was hoping Pouf would follow her, and paused in the doorway to look back at him pleadingly. But the poodle merely gazed at her with an aloof expression in his black shoe-button eyes, and did not move from his position beside his mistress. This morning he seemed to have entirely forgotten that he had jumped up onto Penny's bed last night and curled up in her arms.

Perhaps Aunt Penelope had seen the little girl's longing glance at the dog. She said, "Pouf, you silly fellow, go with Penny."

Pouf stood up, and did as he was told. His manner seemed to say, Very well, if I must. Penny was disappointed that he had not come with her of his own accord; still she was glad to have his company.

"I will be very, very nice and polite to him, and perhaps he will be friendly with me again when he knows me better," she said to herself.

4. BEYOND THE GREEN DOOR

IN THE DAYLIGHT Aunt Penelope's house did not resemble a castle, as it had seemed to in the dusk of evening. It was tall, painted gray, with long narrow windows. The deeply slanting slate roof was peculiar, because it had windows in it too. Here and there the paint was faded and peeling a little. The big house looked rather shabby, though stately and solemn. And the grounds about it, surrounded by the high iron railing, were something like a park—except, alas, that there was no lake, with boats and swans; no wonderful Zoo, with monkeys and lions and bears and brilliant birds. Just mostly trees and grass so smooth and green that Penny supposed she must not walk on it.

So, with Pouf trotting sedately at her heels, she kept to the paths. These were neat and straight, bordered with peculiar foliage that looked as if it had been dusted with flour. The black iron deer stood in a round bed of dark-red spotted plants. At the back of the house was a square space where green shoots, in even rows, poked up through

the dark, moist-looking earth. Penny guessed this must be
a vegetable garden.

She didn't see any flowers growing anywhere, although,
on a small back porch, there was a bright bouquet of them
in a blue-china pitcher beside a green bowl full of apples
and a big book on a table covered with a yellow cloth.
An old rocking-chair stood beside the table, and a bird-
cage hung from the porch ceiling. In it perched a little
brown bird, cocking its head at her, with tiny glittering
black eyes. This little porch was cosy. Penny thought it
was the nicest place, except for the kitchen, that she had
seen.

The large barn, which was some distance from the
house, looked pleasant also, from the outside. It, too, was
painted grey and had wide shallow windows under the overhanging eaves, and a dovecote perched atop the peaked
roof, and a rooster weather-vane. The horse-and-carriage
that had brought them here last night must live in the
barn, and Penny wanted very much to go in. But the big
door was shut tight; she could not even peek inside.

Tucked away in one corner of the grounds beyond a
big, dark-green Christmasy-looking tree and some thick
shrubs, Penny found a little latticed arbor. Vines covered
the top and sides—all except the narrow arched entrance,
and a green-painted weather-stained wooden door at the
far end of the shadowy summer-house.

Penny wondered what was on the other side of the green
door. Would it be all right for her to look? She decided it
would. But when she gave the door a little push it would
not open.

"Perhaps it *pulls* open," she thought, and took hold of the
black-iron door-handle and tugged. The door did not
budge.

Penny sat down on a bench in the summer-house. Pouf

jumped up on the opposite bench. He looked at the little girl gravely, as if he were saying, "Well, what are you going to do next?"

She answered aloud, "There doesn't seem to be *anything* to do." She drew a long breath. "But I can pretend. I'll pretend about what's beyond the green door."

She leaned her cheek on her hand and imagined a lovely garden with roses and hollyhocks and pansies growing beside the winding paths and flowering branches overhanging them; and a sun-dial, and a pool with lilies, and gold-fish, and—"and perhaps a frog—who is really the Frog Prince in disguise! And of course, I'll be the Princess as soon as I step past the door; and Rosmyrelda will be my Lady in Waiting, and Pouf will be a very friendly Dragon who protects me wherever I go. At first, when I sit down beside the pool and the Frog comes up, in his knobby dark skin, staring with his bulgy eyes and saying 'Glub, glub,' Pouf will puff flame and bark at him, 'Go 'way! If you don't, I'll slay you!' But I'll tell him, very nicely, not to bark, that I am not afraid. I'll say, 'Frog, you aren't pretty, but I know you won't hurt me. And I won't hurt you. I really like you, Frog.' And then the Frog will suddenly turn into a beautiful Prince, an awfully nice little boy, with raven locks and silken doublet-and-hose, and he'll smile and tell me how he was enchanted by a Wicked Fairy, and the spell could only be broken when a beautiful little Girl Princess with golden hair spoke kindly to him."

Penny paused for a moment.

"Of course I'm not beautiful and my hair is really straw-colored, not golden, but I can *think* I am and it is." And she went on imagining many more things—how the little Prince taught her to speak with the gold-fish that lived in the pool, and the dragon-flies and butterflies that skimmed over it, and the birds and the flowers too. He had

learned all that, of course, while he was a Frog, under the
Spell of Enchantment.

" 'And it was wonderful to learn it,' " he said, " 'though
the water *was* cold, and I didn't like to be a frog in an ugly
looking green skin who couldn't say anything but glub-
glub. Even though the dragon-flies and the butterflies and
the flowers did know what I meant, it didn't sound pretty,
and I wanted to talk with a human being too. And now I
can talk with you, little Princess. And we can play together
and go on adventures together all over the world! Come."

So they climbed onto a broad pond-lily leaf with turned-
up edges. Of course they had to grow very small to do that,
but as it was an Enchanted Garden they could do it simply
by saying Presto! Naturally Rosmyrelda the Lady-in-Wait-
ing became small too; and Pouf, the Friendly Dragon, was
no bigger than a bumble-bee. They all settled themselves
comfortably on the pond-lily leaf, which flew off, up into
the air and away, as if they were on a Magic Carpet.

They saw many wonderful things; and whenever they
wished to stop the magic leaf floated down, and the Princess Penny and the Prince and Pouf the Good Dragon and
the Lady Rosmyrelda jumped off and had a beautiful time.
They saw windmills, and picked tulips with children in
funny wooden shoes. Then in a flash the scene changed,
it was wintertime, and they all put on silver skates and
skimmed over the frozen canals. After that they went to
the North Pole, where the snow was colored like a rainbow
by the Aurora Borealis, and they talked with friendly white
bears, and when they wanted to warm themselves they
crawled into a little hut that looked like a white-china
sugar-bowl turned upside down, and sat around a fire with
chubby children in furry clothes. In Asia they ate with
chop-sticks and rode in jinrickshas and climbed cherry trees
and heard temple bells; in Paris they lived for a while in

a barge on the River Seine. They visited the Swiss Family Robinson on their Island, and Alice and the Rabbit in Wonderland—and many, many other places.

But after a while Penny's imagination wouldn't take her anywhere else. She looked at Rosmyrelda, who was staring up at the sky with an uninterested expression, and at Pouf, who had put his nose between his paws and closed his eyes.

"I don't believe you've heard a thing I've been thinking," she said, not very kindly. She picked up the doll and gave her a little shake. Pouf opened his eyes, and stretched, and followed at her heels as Penny went slowly back toward the big silent house.

5. WALK RIGHT IN, FOLKS!

SHE SAT ON THE STEPS for a long time—at least it seemed to Penny a very long time—before the door opened and Aunt Penelope said, "Oh, there you are, child! Dinner is ready."

After dinner at the long table in the big gloomy dining-room, Penny sat with Aunt Penelope in the parlor, trying to read her book.

At last her Aunt said, "Excuse me, my dear. I have things to attend to. You may go outdoors again, if you wish. Pouf will go with you."

Penny went outside. Pouf followed. She walked around the house to the barn, but the door was still shut tight. She was tired of the summer-house.

At last she wandered to the big gate in the tall iron railings that fenced the grounds. Outside there was a wide quiet road bordered with trees. There were no people passing, and no house on the other side of the road, only a wide field with hills in the distance.

"But even if there *were* anything interesting to see or do

I couldn't go out," she thought. "Well, I'll try to pretend I'm a Captive, and Aunt Penelope is a Terrible Witch who is keeping me prisoner . . . "

Holding Rosmyrelda in her arms she paced back and forth behind the high railings. But it wasn't a very good "pretend." For one thing, she didn't really like to think of her Aunt as a Witch.

"She isn't truly like one; she's not mean and cross. She —she's just old; too old to like little girls very much, I guess," thought Penny.

She curled up in the shade of a big bush, and shut her eyes, and tried to pretend herself back on the magic pond-lily leaf again. But this time the only place she could make it go was—home. It flew away at once, sailing quickly over the busy city streets, straight to her own red-brick house. Mother and Father were standing on the front stoop, look-ing up eagerly as she swooped down toward them. The next moment she was in their arms, and Mother was saying, "Darling, I've missed you *so* much!" And Father hugged her and said, "You *have* been on an adventure, Pusskin! You must tell us all about it—"

Penny opened her eyes. She couldn't pretend Mother and Father hard enough; she wanted too much for them to be real.

"And I haven't any adventures to tell them—not truly ones," she thought, forlornly. And the prospect of the long empty day stretched ahead—and the night with its lonely country sounds—and the next day—and the next night— forever and ever, it seemed to the little girl—

Suddenly she could not bear it. She jumped up.

"We're going home, Rosmyrelda!" she said firmly.

She hurried back to the house and in the front door quietly, and tip-toed across the dim hall up the stairs to her room. She did not want to meet Aunt Penelope; it would be too hard to explain how she felt, and probably her Aunt would not let her go.

"But of course I must leave her a letter, so she won't think I've just run away, and be worried," she told herself.

Mother had given her a little box of note-paper with forget-me-nots printed in one corner, on which to write letters home; she got this from her satchel, took out the pink pencil that went with it, and wrote:

> Dear Aunt Penelope, I am going home, please don't worry, I have a dollar Father gave me, it will pay for the train ticket. Please excuse me. Your niece, Penny.

She pinned the message to her pillow, and put on her straw "country" hat. She decided not to change her dress, or wear her reefer—it was such a warm day. And she knew she would have to walk quite a long way to the depot; her valise would be too heavy to carry that far.

"But I had better take my umbrella, in case it rains. And something to eat, because I may get hungry," she said to herself, remembering the apple and the chocolate she had not eaten on the train. So she wrapped the apple and the chocolate in a colored kerchief she had brought with her, knotting the corners together so that it made a kind of bag. At the last minute she remembered to tuck her red purse in her pocket, and with Rosmyrelda under one arm and her lunch and umbrella under the other she stole downstairs and out of the house.

Her heart was beating fast with excitement as she hurried down the front path and slipped through the big gate. Her conscience hurt her a little, too.

"I know Aunt Penelope told me not to 'go outside the gate to play'—but I'm not going out to *play*. And I just couldn't stay, all the time—all alone. I'm sure Mother and Father will understand. And it will be so wonderful to be home!"

The thought made her so happy that her legs in their ribbed white stockings went very fast; she had soon passed the railing that enclosed her Aunt's big house.

She said to herself, "Father will write to Aunt, and tell her I'm safe and sound, and explain that I've never been away from home before in all my life. But I do wish I'd said goodbye to Pouf. Perhaps he'll jump on my bed tonight—and I won't be there." Still, he had not followed when she had gone into the house for her belongings, and when she came out he was nowhere in sight. "So maybe he won't really miss me," she thought.

Just at this moment she heard a short sharp bark and a sound of small quick footsteps. She turned around—and there was the poodle, running toward her!

As he reached her Penny stooped quickly; she wanted to pick the little dog up and hug him as she said goodbye. But he drew back, and sat down. His pink tongue was hanging out; he had run very fast, but he still looked haughty—and reproachful, Penny thought. He stared up at her with his solemn black eyes, and gave another short bark.

"Perhaps he is scolding me. Or maybe that is his word for 'goodbye,' " Penny thought. "I wish I knew."

Aloud she said, "Well, goodbye, Pouf. I like you very much already, and I wish we had time to become intimate friends. I wish you could come home with me, but of course you cannot leave *your* home." She reached for his paw, shook it politely, then gave it a little squeeze. "Well, goodbye again."

She stood up and went on again. The little dog followed.

Penny stopped. "Pouf," she said, "I suppose you think I am just going for a walk, and you want to come too. But you can't, you see, because I am going home. So you must go back to Aunt Penelope. Don't you understand?"

She pointed in the direction of her Aunt's house, and said, "Go, Pouf! Go back, now!"

But the little dog did not move. And when Penny turned and walked on again, he trotted sedately beside her.

Though she hated to do it, this time Penny scolded him. But when she continued on her way, he went with her.

"Oh dear, what shall I do! I would love to have you come with me, Pouf, but it wouldn't be right." Then she had a sudden thought. "Perhaps you just want to come with me to see me to the train, to see me off!" she said. "Is that it, Pouf?"

The poodle barked, once.

"I hope that means Yes," said Penny. She added, "And are you sure you can find your way back home again to Aunt?"

Pouf did not reply. But Penny had often heard that dogs could find their way back to their homes even from long distances. Consoling herself with this thought she went on, with the poodle beside her. It was, of course, very pleasant to have his company.

Happily, she picked a black-eyed susan and stuck it in the ribbon on her hat.

"Perhaps we'll have a really truly adventure on the way —so I'll have something to tell Father all about!" she said. "And I guess, Pouf, that we're quite intimate friends already. Even if you are such a dignified little dog, and not used to being petted and hugged, you do seem to like me. I'll be sorry when we reach the depot and I have to leave you."

At the thought she felt quite a pang. But the next moment she forgot this. For they were passing a rambling white house surrounded by a picket fence; and in the yard, to one side of the house, was a tent made of two torn sheets, a ragged blanket and an old quilt. In front of the tent stood a boy in overalls—a barefooted boy with red hair and freckles. He had on a pointed hat made of newspaper with a feather stuck in it, and he was shouting in a loud singsong:

"Walk right in, folks! Walk right in! Only two pins to see the circus! Just step this way to see the show and get your refresh-ments—lemonade only one penny, peanuts two cents! The show is about to start—don't miss Wonderful Willie and Tillie the Tiger and Joe the Strong Man! Also acrobats and clowns! And Mister Mike, the Marvelous Magician! Co-o-me *right* in, folks! This way!"

Penny hesitated only for an instant.

"I don't know when the train goes, so there's no use hurrying to catch it," she remarked to herself as she opened the gate in the picket fence and went in.

6. SUNSHINE AND RAIN

"I'M AFRAID I haven't any pins, but perhaps you will let me pay to see the circus with pennies instead. And I'd like some peanuts, too, please," she said to the freckled boy.

"Certainly, lady, certainly! Here you are—fresh roasted peanuts!" he said in a deep voice, and handed her a small bag of peanuts with a flourish. Then he added in his regular boy's voice, "They aren't exac'ly just-right-now fresh-roasted. I been saving 'em ever since the real circus was here. Because you *gotta* have peanuts at *any* circus."

"Yes, of course," nodded Penny, as she took out her purse and handed the boy two cents. She herself had been taken to the circus in Madison Square Garden every year since she was five years old, so she understood that what the boy said was certainly so. She was very eager indeed to see this circus; but as she started to give the boy two more pennies instead of pins he shook his head.

"No-o, that wouldn't be fair. I said two pins, so I can't take money." He frowned, and Penny's heart sank.

Then the boy's face brightened. "But I tell you what!" he said. "The pins are supposed to be pennies anyway, so you can just give me some pretend money. That'll be just as good."

"Why, certainly," said Penny. She put the pennies back in her purse, and taking out some pretend money handed it to him with an elegant gesture.

"Have you change for a dollar, Mister?" she asked in a ladyish, slightly through-her-nose voice. "This is for myself and Miss Rosmyrelda too."

"Certainly, lady! Plenty of change!" the boy replied in his deep "mannish" voice, and bowed as he took the "dollar" and put it in his pocket. He drew out some pretend change, counted it carefully out on his palm and gave it to her. "Here you are, lady!"

Penny closed her fist on it tightly, then opened her fingers and stuffed the "money" in her purse.

"Thank you," she said.

She looked at the pitcher of lemonade that stood on a soapbox counter, beside three more little bags of peanuts. It was very tempting.

"I would like some lemonade, too, if there is time before the circus begins," she said.

"Plenty of time, lady, plenty of time!" said the boy in his "mannish" voice.

This time she paid with a real copper coin, and as he filled a glass and handed it to her he added, "My Gramp gave me the lemons and sugar; it's good lemonade." He added, "I'm saving up for some skates."

The lemonade was very good, Penny thought. As she was drinking it there was a sudden commotion within the tent; several short barks and a loud "miouw!" Penny looked quickly around—could it be Pouf barking? But Pouf was sitting sedately in the shade of a nearby bush. And just then a large striped-yellow cat, its tail bristling, darted out from under the tent and dashed away. Pouf turned to watch it, but did not move.

"Gosh, there goes Tillie. Willie musta jumped at her. He does it just for fun but she doesn't like it," said the red-haired boy. "Well, Tillie's not much of a tiger anyhow. Ole thing just sits and washes herself—or sleeps. I can't teach her a trick, she's too lazy. But I guess Willie's getting sorta restless, so maybe the circus better start. That is, when you've finished your lemonade," he added politely.

Penny finished the last swallow and set the glass down. The boy gestured grandly toward the open side of the tent and bowed as he said, deep in his throat, "Just step this way, lady! Walk right in!"

As Penny did so Pouf got up, giving himself a shake, and followed her.

"Oh, excuse me, I must pay for my friend to see the circus too!" she said. When she had paid she was led to a seat on a long board resting on two boxes. Pouf sat beside her, with Rosmyrelda next to him, and the circus began.

First, however, the boy went to a little dog which was tied to one of the clothes-lines that held up the tent, and patted his head.

"Now, Willie, you be good. Your act doesn't begin yet. I gotta do mine first, then it'll be your turn. So you just sit still. Behave, now!"

The little dog licked the boy's hand and smiled. He wagged his tail very hard, then sat down on it. The tip of his tongue showed, and he seemed breathless with excitement as his large brown eyes followed every move his master made.

Penny felt much the same way as the boy announced: "Ladies *and* gentlemen, you will now see Joe the Strong Man! The strongest man in the world! He can pick up a

hundred pounds—why, I guess he could pick up a million pounds, or maybe even a—a billion! Now, watch!—This is Joe," he added, bowing.

He rolled up his sleeves, and slowly lifted a large red ball from the ground. Anyone could tell from the way he tugged and grunted and puffed out his cheeks that the ball was terribly heavy.

"Why, it probably weighs more than a quadrillion pounds!" Penny said softly to Pouf and Rosmyrelda. "And look—*now* he's holding it 'way over his head—with only one hand!"

After that came "The Great Acrobatic Act," which was even more exciting. The acrobat stood on his head, turned somersaults and handsprings. "And I can hang from my knees, too, only there isn't anything here to hang from," he remarked.

Next came "Mike the Marvelous Magician," who wore a falseface with a red nose and curly black moustache, a shiny high hat, and tossed copper coins up in the air, then pulled them right out of Willie's long silky ears. Mike took them out of his own ears too, and finally even one from Rosmyrelda's gingham lap.

Then it was Wonderful Willie's turn, and no one could deny that Willie deserved his name! First he sat up, holding up both paws and smiling. At the command to "Speak!" he spoke—three short barks. He lay still as a mouse when he was told to, rolled over when the word was given, walked, and even *danced* around on his hind legs while his master beat time on a tambourine, and finally, at the snap of a finger, jumped through a hoop!

"And that's all, ladies and gentlemen!" said the proprietor of the Circus.

Penny sighed and unclasped her hands. Then she remembered to clap them. She had been too spellbound to applaud

before. Her eyes were shining as she said, "It was a perfectly beautiful circus!"

She gathered up her kerchief and her umbrella and Rosmyrelda.

"Well, goodbye," she said.

"Well, goodbye," said the boy.

Penny went on her way again, Pouf trotting beside her. As she walked she kept thinking of the circus.

"It was the nicest one I ever saw," she said. "But," she added, to the poodle, "I don't believe you appreciated it at all! I noticed, once or twice, that you looked quite supe —supercilious! Especially when it was Wonderful Willie's turn. You looked as if you thought you could do all his tricks much better, if you *wanted* to! Well, perhaps you could. But just the same, it isn't very polite to put your nose up in the air the way you did. Willie was awfully nice. And so was that boy."

The truth was, she couldn't help feeling a little sad because she was going away and would never see the freckled boy again. Soon, too, she began to feel a little tired. She wished she had asked the boy the way to the depot; when she had started out she had been quite sure which direction to take, but now she was less certain.

"Perhaps I'm hungry, too," she said, and as she was passing a wide meadow she decided it would be a good place to stop and eat her lunch. She found a tiny bit of shade near a bush, sat down and unfastened the colored kerchief. She unwrapped the silver foil from the little slab of chocolate and shared it with Pouf. She offered him part of the apple, too, but he did not want it, so she slowly munched it herself, right down to the core.

The meadow was full of wild flowers such as Penny had

only seen in pictures and dreamed of. (In her own back
yard at home there were just a few spindly geraniums.)
So she made Pouf a necklace of daisies and buttercups and
other lovely blossoms, pink and purple and blue; and she
gathered a bouquet to take home. While she picked the
flowers she made believe that she was in a wide wild garden,
and the red-haired boy was there too, and she was a Princess and he was a Prince. She called him Prince Golden
Freckles, and made up a long story about his Gramp, whom
she named King Percival Malcolm Almonde Freckles.

It was such a lovely story that she lay down in the bright
tall grass to continue with it. There were big grey and
white clouds in the sky, but the sun was hot and shone
in her eyes, so she opened her umbrella and propped it
against the bush to shade her face. Her silk kerchief was
empty now, so she spread it over Pouf, who had curled
up beside her. She held Rosmyrelda in her arms. After
awhile she fell asleep, though she did not mean to and
had no idea that she had done so, until—

Suddenly she heard a funny sound, almost in her ear.
"Mooooo!" was what she heard.

She opened her eyes and blinked them.

From behind the bush and the umbrella poked a shiny
wet black nose. Two large soft dark eyes were gazing at her
with great curiosity.

She sat up, staring at a little white calf with tan-colored
spots and gangling legs. A butterfly with black and orange
wings had been resting on the posy in Penny's hat. It fluttered away when she moved. Pouf woke up too, and seeing
the calf, planted his feet firmly, thrusting out his long thin
jaw. His ruff stuck out even more stiffly than usual and
his tail, with the round tuft at the end of it, was like a
small ramrod. "Grrrrr!" he said. Quite plainly he considered the calf a dangerous interloper.

Penny was not frightened; she had always wanted to meet a little calf. She put her arm around Pouf and said, "Shhsh. He won't hurt us."

But the poodle's small body remained tense under her arm.

"Grrrrrr—yap-yap—wow-*wow*-WOW!" he barked.

"Moo—*ooo*—OOOO!" answered the calf. And from some-where, somewhere quite close by, came an answering, low-toned but loud bellow: "Moo—ooo—OOOOO!"

Penny jumped to her feet. Just behind the little gentle calf was a large—a very large—cow. Or—or was it a bull? It was walking slowly toward them.

Penny had heard that bulls didn't like red. She glanced down at the red tassels on her black buttoned shoes, and at the red bow that tied up Pouf's frizzy bangs. She tucked Rosmyrelda in the red gingham dress under her pinafore and snatched up the kerchief that had a pattern of red circles on it. Telling Pouf to be calm, and using her open umbrella as a shield, she backed away through the meadow toward the road. Reaching it, she scurried off.

The calf and its protector did not follow. Soon Penny slacked her pace. She felt a bit silly; maybe the bull wasn't one at all, but just the calf's mother, coming to look after him.

"Probably we're just 'fraidy-cats, Pouf," she said.

At that moment a large drop of rain splashed on her nose. She looked up and saw what she hadn't had time to notice since the calf had waked her up—the big grey clouds had spread all over the sky. Another drop followed the first, plopping right into her eye as she gazed upward. Then they began to come down faster and faster. In the distance, thunder rumbled, and a gust of wind blew Penny's hat right off her head.

She ran after it, put it on and tied it down with her

colored silk kerchief. "It's a good thing I have my umbrella!" she said. "Come, Pouf, keep under it." But the
little dog, trotting on ahead of her, didn't seem to mind
the rain at all.

"Well, *you've* got a fine fur coat, but I haven't!" said
Penny. She hurried on as fast as she could go. Would she
never come to the depot? On and on and on she walked.
The rain came down harder and harder, making puddles
in the road. Some of them were so big that she had to
slosh right through them; the water soaked through her
shoes so that they went squelch-squelch at every step; their
pretty red tassels were limp and her white stockings spat-
tered with mud. In spite of the umbrella her sprigged green
gingham frock and her pinafore were damp and bedraggled. She was cold and shivering as she plodded on. And it
was growing darker and darker.

"Maybe the sun has gone down and it will soon be night
time," she thought. The sky was so black with clouds that
she really couldn't tell. And she had to keep the umbrella
close down over her head and watch her feet in order not
to step into too many muddy puddles. She could hardly
tell where she was going. "But I ought to be there *soon,*"
she said, through chattering teeth.

"Bow WOW!" said Pouf, as if in answer.

He turned sharply to the left, and darted off. Penny
looked—and saw that she was in front of the big iron gate
to her Aunt Penelope's house. Apparently, after the calf
had waked her and she'd run away frightened, she had
started right back—the way she had come! And now she
was too cold and wet, it was too rainy and dark and late to
turn around and try to find her way to the depot.

She pushed open the gate and walked up the graveled
path toward the front porch and the lights beside the big
mahogany door.

Pouf was already there, barking several short sharp barks. "I hope Aunt Penelope won't be *very* cross at me," thought Penny as she stumbled up the steps.

7. AUNTIE'S MUD PIES

THE DOOR OPENED wide before Penny reached it. Her Aunt stood there with Mister Jonah, holding a lamp, just behind her. When she saw Penny she cried, "My dear—oh, my dear!" and ran to her.

"You've come back!" she said, her arms around the little girl. "Oh darling, I'm so glad! I'm so sorry. . . . I mean I'm so—so—"

She pressed her soft wrinkled cheek against Penny's rain-wet face. And at that moment, at the moment when her Aunt's arms went closely around her and her voice was warm and free, Penny suddenly understood.

She clasped her hands tightly about her Aunt's neck and buried her nose against her.

"I'm sorry, too," she whispered. Then she looked up at the little wrinkled old face bending over her. It wasn't solemn and stand-offish any more. Nor, she could tell, was her own face. She smiled all over as she said, "And glad, too. You—you do love me, don't you, Auntie?"

"My darling, I've loved you—and wanted to hug you and pet you from the very first minute you got off the train —and long before!" said Aunt Penelope. "Only—I didn't know if you'd want me to—I wasn't sure that you'd like *me*—"

"Oh, but I do!" said Penny. And she did. She liked the soft blue eyes, the cheeks like crinkled wild-rose petals, the silvery curls on each side of them. She touched one with a finger. "You—you're cute," she whispered.

But warm and happy as she felt inside, she couldn't keep her teeth from chattering.

"I'm a dummy, that's what I am!" cried Aunt Penelope. "You're wet and cold!—Jonah, get the big granite pan and fill it with hot water and put it front of the kitchen range. Hurry, now!"

A few minutes later Penny was sitting in the warm bright kitchen with her feet in a hot mustard bath. Aunt Penelope had taken off her wet pinafore and frock and her shoes and stockings, and bundled a thick patchwork quilt around her. She held Rosmyrelda in her arms, and Pouf dozed nearby, wrapped in a red woolen shawl. Aunt Penelope bustled around the stove, which glowed pleasantly; and Mister Jonah, a teacloth tied 'round his middle, pottered about, helping. A delicious smell of hot food cooking filled the room. Penny felt drowsy and content.

Afterwards she found that she was very hungry too—in spite of the lemonade and peanuts, the apple and the bits of chocolate she had shared with Pouf. After all, she hadn't been able to eat much supper yesterday, or much breakfast or dinner today, she had been so lonesome and homesick. But now, with her chair moved close to her Aunt's—and a hassock on it to lift her to a more comfortable height— everything tasted good. She had two helpings of creamed chicken and dumplings, and told her Aunt, between

mouthfuls, about her adventures; with the barefooted boy
and his circus, and Wonderful Willie and Tillie the Tiger;
and the little calf that had come to find out who was eating
lunch and picking flowers and falling asleep in *his* meadow!

"And maybe," she added, "he would have liked to play
with Pouf and Rosmyrelda and me and felt disappointed
when we ran away. But his mother—or father, whichever
it was—didn't *seem* very welcoming—and was awfully big!
Well anyway, even if I was a silly 'fraid-cat to run away I'm
not sorry. Because if I hadn't been scared I mightn't have
got all mixed-up and turned around so that I came back
from where I started; and I'm glad I did."

"So am I, darling," said her Aunt.

Penny finished her last spoonful of custard.

"My, that was good," she sighed. "All velvety, and it had
such a lot of special little different tastes—and smells—in
it!"

Her Aunt beamed. "Well, I used honey in it instead of
sugar, that makes it smooth. And there's lemon, and just
a tiny bit of almond, and cinnamon. It's one of my experi-
ments, Jonah calls them my 'mud-pies.' But he likes them
too."

She hesitated, then continued, leaning across the table
and whispering almost guiltily, "I've always loved to cook!
When I was little I used to steal into the kitchen to watch,
and Hetty, our colored mammy, let me help too. But one
day my mother found me there and scolded me. She said
the kitchen was no place for a little lady, and I would waste
the food and Hetty's time and spoil my hands and learn
bad manners. I cried, and she was very disappointed with
me and wouldn't speak to me for a whole week. So I never
went into the kitchen again until I was quite grown up.
And even then—even now—when I put on an apron and
putter around with my pots and pans having a beautiful

time, sometimes all of a sudden I feel—quite naughty! As
if I were being a disobedient little girl and Mother might
come in the door and find me out! So, you see, nobody but
Jonah—and now you, Penny—knows how I like to bake pies
and biscuits and cake."

Penny knew what an important secret had just been
shared with her. She realized too why she had been ordered
so sharply out of the kitchen that morning.

She nodded thoughtfully.

"Sometimes grown-up people have funny ideas, don't
they?" she said thoughtfully. "My Mother won't let me have
roller-skates because she had a sister who hurt herself roller-
skating when she was little." She sighed, then brightened
up. "But she likes me to learn to do 'most everything else
—read and paint and sing and play the piano and sew and
cook. So—tomorrow, Auntie, will you let me help you make
'mud-pies?' " Her eyes crinkled.

Her Aunt laughed and promised, and after that Mister
Jonah came in to clear the table and they went into the
parlor.

But tonight it was no longer gloomy there. The little fire
burned merrily, and looking around the room Penny saw
many things that interested her. On a low marble ledge
beneath a tall gilt mirror there was a huge shell, intricately
curved and delicately fluted, tinted inside like a rose. Aunt
Penelope told her to hold it close to her ear and hark!
Could she hear the sea?

She listened, and she did! A low lisping murmur, the
waves slipping up the wet sand on silver tiptoes. Then she
pressed the shell closer and the ocean surged and boomed.
And underneath there were voices—

"I can hear the mermaids, too!" she said.

She put the sea shell to her Aunt's ear.

"Oh." Aunt Penelope's blue eyes were wide.

After they had listened to the shell a while longer Penny put it back. "What are these, Auntie?" she asked, touching the tall bronze feathers that stood in a blue Chinese vase in front of the mirror.

"They are peacock feathers," answered Aunt Penelope, and told her the story of Argus and his hundred eyes.

And then she told Penny a lovely story about the Dresden shepherd and shepherdess smiling to one another from either end of the long mantelpiece. The little girl was curled up on the hearthrug with Pouf at her feet. She leaned her head against her Aunt's knee, and the loving old fingers smoothed her hair gently.

She looked all around the room: at the shadowy portraits and silhouettes and miniatures and samplers against the faded wallpaper, the shelves of old books, the sofa-cushions embroidered in beads and the needlework rugs; at glass domes gleaming like soapbubbles shielding wax fruit, a basket of iridescent shells, a little green-and-red-and-yellow bird perched on a twig, a bouquet of flowers made out of feathers.

On top of a corner what-not a small ship sailed, caged within a bottle of bluish glass; on the shelves beneath it were tiny ivory figures, exquisite outspread fans from China, Japan, France, and Spain, shells, coral, an Indian tomahawk, a collection of butterflies framed under glass and an elephant's tusk. A harp stood beside a small parlor organ at one end of the room.

How different from last night everything seemed!

Penny said softly, "I guess you could tell a million stories about the things in this room, couldn't you, Auntie? And there's a special one I want right now, please!"

She jumped up and opened the big family album. Aunt Penelope drew her chair closer to the table as Penny quickly turned the pages until she found the one she wanted.

This held the daguerreotype of a little snub-nosed girl in a plaid hoop-skirt with ruffled pantellettes showing beneath it. The picture had been faintly tinted and the child's straight long hair was pale yellow and held back from her forehead by a blue ribbon that matched her round grave eyes.

"Who is she, Auntie?" asked Penny. "She—she looks like me, doesn't she?" she added.

Aunt Penelope smiled and nodded. "Yes, I believe she does."

"Please tell me about her!" urged Penny.

"Well—let's see—" Aunt Penelope paused, and Penny knew she was thinking how to begin the story. Finally she turned the album pages back to a picture of a stern-faced lady in a stiff elaborate black dress, and another of a handsome jolly looking gentleman in a uniform.

"That was the little girl's mamma, and that was her papa," she said. "He went away to fight in the Mexican Wars when she was a baby, and he never came back. After that the little girl's Mamma was never very well or very happy."

Quickly she found the portrait of a smiling dark-haired boy.

"That is the little girl's brother. They had wonderful times together when they were young. Then he grew up and went away and married; but he sent her his own little son to take care of for a while, and they, too, had beautiful good times. This is *his* picture."

Gently her finger touched the photograph of another small boy, as she said, "That is your father."

"Then—then that little girl is—you! Isn't she?" said Penny.

Aunt Penelope nodded. Just then the clock struck nine, and she exclaimed, "Come darling! Meshak, Shadrach— and to-bed-we-go!"

She closed the album and they went upstairs arm in arm.

A little later, when Penny was ready for bed, she knelt down at Aunt Penelope's knee and said her prayers:

"Now I lay me down to sleep, I pray the Lord my soul to keep. Please bless Mother and Father and Auntie, and Pouf and Mister Jonah, and the red-headed boy, and Willie." She hesitated, then added something that had been on her mind, "And—and the old gentleman on the train. I was rude to him, and I'm afraid I hurt his feelings. I'm sorry. Amen."

She scurried up the little ladder into bed, and Aunt Penelope tucked the covers around her. She opened the window, and asked, "Shall I leave the night-light burning?"

"Oh no, I like the dark when I'm happy," answered Penny.

Her Aunt blew out the lamp and snuffed the wick. She kissed the little girl, smoothed the quilt tenderly. Penny put out her hand and reached for Aunt Penelope's.

"I didn't tell you about the old man who tried to be friends with me, on the train, did I?" she said. "I knew

he meant to be kind; but I *was* crying—just a little bit—though I was pretending not to. So I didn't answer him and I guess I seemed very cross. You know, Auntie, I had that—that sort of curled-up feeling inside, that I get when I don't know people very well."

"I know, dear," said her Aunt.

Penny sighed. "Do you think we can get over it, if we try very hard?" she asked earnestly.

Aunt Penelope knew that she had missed a great deal of happiness in her life because she had not conquered her shyness, but she did not say that; and she truly felt hopeful. She answered gravely, "We will certainly try, won't we?"

Penny nodded. "I've never talked to anyone about it before," she whispered, "not even my Father. And he's so jolly and wise too—I expect that's the only thing he mightn't understand about. Of course he wouldn't laugh at me, but I'm afraid he would *think* it was silly."

She snuggled down under the covers, and Aunt Penelope kissed her goodnight and went softly away, leaving the door ajar.

A moment later Penny heard the tap-tap-tap of Pouf's footsteps and felt the small kerplunk as the little dog landed on the bed. She put her arm around him, and shut her eyes.

On the porch roof outside the bedroom windows the rain fell gently. She wondered if it would still be raining the next morning. "But I won't mind if it does. We'll make 'mud-pies,' and tell stories, and perhaps Auntie will teach me how to crochet and I'll make a little hug-me-tight for Mother and a muffler for Father. And . . . and . . . " Soon she was fast asleep.

8.   ENCHANTED GARDEN

THE RAIN HAD STOPPED when Penny woke up, and a gay breeze fluttered the dimity window curtains, bringing fresh lovely smells to Penny's nose.

She bathed and dressed in a great hurry, and ran downstairs and straight to the kitchen.

"Ho, lazybones, so you're up at last!" said Aunt Penelope, who was stirring batter in a big yellow bowl. "Why, Pouf has been to wake you twice! Each time he came down shaking his head, saying that when he peeked in you looked too comfortable to disturb! Hmmmph."

Penny glanced at the poodle, who sat before the stove looking dignified and aloof as usual (except at night-time, thought Penny with happy amusement.) She suspected that Aunt Penelope herself had been the one who'd peeked in.

"Good morning, Mister Jonah!" she said blithely, and the old man grinned as he replied.

Aunt Penelope gave her the batter to stir while she greased a big iron griddle, and afterwards showed her just how to ladle out smooth, creamy spoonfuls and drop them on the shining black surface of the griddle. And when to turn them—when the little bubbles popped up in the thin round cakes—and how to slide the pancake-turner underneath and flip them quickly over.

How delicious they were, brown and smoking hot and covered with butter and maple syrup! Even the first two that Penny had made tasted good, though their edges were a bit ragged and they were a little—well, quite a little browner than they were supposed to be. Aunt Penelope said they were exceptional for a first attempt, and that Penny had a "light hand," she could see.

There were baked apples too for breakfast; and they ate on the little back porch, on the table covered with the yellow cloth. The small bird in his cage cocked his head at them. Aunt Penelope said that his name was Cherky; she'd found him, after a rainstorm, lying on the grass, hurt. She showed Penny the tiny splint she'd made, still binding the broken wing. But it would be well soon, and then they'd open the cage and Cherky would fly away.

"Do you think he'll go far away—forever?" asked Penny wistfully.

"Well, of course I hope he'll build a nest right nearby," admitted Aunt Penelope. "But anyway his children are pretty sure to come back some day. As a matter of fact, I believe it was his great-great-great-great-great-grandpapa, Chipsey, whose broken leg your Father mended when he was a boy. That was—let's see, it was more than twenty years ago! But Chirky's likeness to Chipsey is remarkable. You see that tiny diamond-shaped black spot on his head, and those markings on the tips of his wings? He has the same disposition, too; cheerful and saucy. And—"

"And I believe he's heard the story of his great-great-great-great-great-great-grandfather before—handed down through the family, you know!" exclaimed Penny, pointing to the little bird. "Look! He's listening to every word we say!" She clasped her hands and said eagerly, "Oh, Aunt Penelope, please tell me some more about my Father when he was a little boy!"

So her Aunt told her about those happy long-ago years; at least they seemed long-ago to Penny, until, as her Aunt talked, she could almost see the blue-eyed, brown-faced boy, with "a thatch of black curls that never would stay tidy, and a big smile that—well, that made you simply have to smile back—"

"Just the way it does now," breathed Penny.

"He was only five years old when they brought him to me, and not very strong; you see, his father (my brother Thomas) had a coffee plantation in Brazil, and the climate didn't agree with the little fellow. But he soon grew sturdy here, and what fun we had in those next four years! Then his mother and father moved back to this country, and of course he went to live with them again."

Aunt Penelope went on to tell about Snicker, the pony, and Bluff, the big Saint Bernard, and Skeeter, the terrier —who had been the boy's companions. Of sleigh rides in

the snowy winter, and climbing cherry-trees and going fishing in summer; of Tommy's first—and last—"fisticuffs,"
when he came home with his coatsleeve and one tooth
gone—

"But dat toof was loose anyway," said old Jonah. "And
dat other boy was a head taller'n Tommy, and a bully, an'
he sho' got de wust of it!" He began to clear the breakfast
dishes away. "He neber teched ou' boy agin.—An' don'
fo'git to tell how de li'l imp skeered me wid dat punkin'
face he carved on Hallowe'en. And de way we played Injun,
hidin' behin' trees and jumpin' out wid war-whoops, hol-
lerin' like to raise de roof! An' how you-all had treasure
hunts an' played hide-and-seek all ober de house on rainy
days. My, my! Dem was libely times." He chuckled and
shuffled off with his laden tray.

Aunt Penelope nodded. "But Tommy could be quiet and
earnest too. He was good at his school work—except spell-
ing—and he liked to read, and he loved to draw and paint."
Suddenly she looked at the gold watch she wore tucked in
her belt and exclaimed, "Mercy me, it's after nine o'clock!"
She popped up out of her rocking chair, which almost fell
over backward.

"Oh," cried Penny, "please tell me more!"

"Indeed I will, but not now," said her Aunt. "It's high
time we got at our 'mud-pies!' "

So they went into the kitchen, where Aunt Penelope let
Penny measure and sift flour, and showed her how to
break the eggs neatly and pour the yolks back and forth
into the open shells, letting the whites fall into a bowl
where they were whipped into a sparkling fluff, like sea-
form. She showed her how to cream the golden butter, with
suger and spices. And how to heat and stir the chocolate
for icing, and test it by dripping it from the point of a
spoon until it was exactly right—neither too thick nor too

thin. They made two kinds of pie, and cookies and a chocolate layer cake. Afterwards Penny scraped the mixing-bowls, licking the spoons. And when everything was done and the kitchen spic-and-span again they went off to the barn to visit Prince, the brown horse.

The barn was big and dusky, and smelled of leather and horses, old wood, and hay and apples. Besides the carriage she had already ridden in there was an older one like a small ancient stagecoach, and a farm wagon. There were wheel-barrows, garden tools, all sorts of odds and ends, and a narrow ladder leading up to the hay-loft. The sunbeams slanting across the shady depths of the barn were filled with tiny dust-flecks—like golden snowflakes.

"What a wonderful place to play—or have a *circus*," thought Penny. Then she forgot everything else as Prince whinnied and poked his face. with a white star in the middle of his forehead, over his stall.

Aunt Penelope introduced them to one another, and Penny stroked him and fed him an apple and a lump of sugar. She watched while Mister Jonah curried the sleek coat until it gleamed. He promised to teach her how to do it, and also to ride Prince, who was very gentle.

"But not dis mo'nin' 'cause Ah got mah veg-tables to hoe. De weeds am acreepin' up on me," said the old man.

They left him in the vegetable garden, where Penny learned that the green rows she had seen yesterday were onions, radishes, parsley, beans, peas, corn, squash, turnips and tomatoes and cucumbers and cabbage and cauliflower and pumpkins.

Afterwards, back in the house, she helped her Aunt make their beds and dust the parlor. They shared the work, so it was finished quickly.

"Now," said Aunt Penelope, "we have a whole beautiful hour before dinnertime. What would you like best to do?"

Penny thought it over. Then she said slowly, "Is the Green Door a—a secret?"

"Yes," said Aunt Penelope, "it is. No one really knows all about it, except me. But—now it will be *our* secret. Just yours and mine."

They walked down the path together and through the summerhouse, and Aunt Penelope took a key out of her pocket and unlocked the Green Door.

Penny stood and gazed around her.

She was in the very garden she had dreamed of! Here

were the winding paths overhung with sweet-scented flowering branches, the little pool with pond-lilies, the sundial, the roses, and a lovely wild tangle of flowers—more different kinds of flowers than Penny had ever seen or imagined.

As they wandered through the fragrant jungle Aunt Penelope told the little city girl the names of the flowers, or of the green leaves where flowers had already bloomed, or would soon blossom. There were lilies-of-the-valley, and iris, and daffodils—"daffy-down-dillies," Aunt Penelope called them. And pansies, "Johnny-jump-ups." And dusty miller (that was the flour-sprinkled foliage she had seen before, along the paths outside,) and mignonette and verbena and prince's feather. "And see, these will be marigolds —my father used to call them marybuds. And later there will be dahlias and chrysanthemums and asters—'Michaelmas daisies' they're called in England. It will be cold before they bloom," said Aunt Penelope.

"And I won't be here then," said Penny wistfully. She gazed around the enchanted garden. She felt that she never wanted to leave it.

"But," said Aunt Penelope, "you are here this minute. And you can always remember it, too."

"Yes, I will," said Penny.

9. HELLO, CALEB!

THAT AFTERNOON they went for a drive, through a covered bridge over a stream, to the village store, which seemed to sell everything—calico and candy, buttons and boots and bacon, sugar and salt and shoe-strings and soap. Aunt Penelope made some purchases, while Penny sniffed the strange spicy mixed-up smell of the small shop. And on the way home she held the reins and Mister Jonah showed her how to guide Prince.

After supper, which she helped Aunt Penelope to prepare, her Aunt brought out a checkered board and taught her to play Lotto, and even though Penny was learning her Aunt never let her win on purpose, so it was lots of fun.

The next morning was rainy, and they explored the attic. What wonderful things they discovered! There was a spinning-wheel, and a uniform that had belonged to Penny's Grandfather who had been in the Civil War; a wax doll and rush-bottomed chair that had been Great-Grandmother's; and a round-topped brass-bound trunk covered with horse-

hair and holding a tiny parasol, a lace shawl, and a flowered silk gown with a skirt that was yards and yards around.

Penny dressed up in the gown, draped the shawl around her and held the parasol over her shoulder and paraded around the attic. Aunt Penelope opened a bandbox and took out a posy-lined poke-bonnet and tied the ribbons under Penny's chin.

"Now you're Great-Grandmother Marie Ann Penelope Elizabeth. Look!" she said, and pointed to an old mirror in one corner of the garret.

Penny looked, and even in the cracked dusty mirror she thought she looked very nice—and strange and different—in the trailing frock and the deep bonnet. She turned and twirled in a little dance.

"May I dress up in it again often?" she asked.

"Yes, whenever you like," said her Aunt. She was burrowing in another trunk. "See here what I've found!" she cried.

"What?" Penny turned to look.

Her Aunt was holding up a small pair of faded and patched blue overalls.

"They were Tommy's—your Father's. The first pair he ever had!"

Penny took them and held them up in front of her. They looked very comical in front of her ladylike costume, but she wasn't thinking of that. "Look, Auntie!" she exclaimed, "They're *just* the right size for me! May I put them on?"

Her Aunt laughed and nodded, and Penny climbed quickly out of her long skirts and into the little blue overalls. They fitted her very well. She looked down at her legs and giggled. Then she thrust her hands in her pockets and strutted up and down.

"Now I'm Father—I mean Tommy!" she laughed. And added, after a moment, "Auntie, couldn't I wear these and help Mister Jonah weed his garden in them? It would keep my stockings clean. And—and besides, I like them."

Aunt Penelope hesitated. In those days little girls didn't wear overalls and the idea was rather startling. But after a moment she said stoutly, "Well, I don't see why not!" She laughed. "Though I'm afraid poor old Jonah will be pretty flabbergasted!"

Which he was. But he soon got used to Penny's small figure in the old blue overalls, kneeling beside him and "rootin' out dem pesky weeds." And Penny loved the smell of the moist rich earth as she worked beside the old man, between the long even rows of green growing vegetables.

She helped in Aunt Penelope's secret garden behind the Green Gate, too. And climbed trees, and learned to ride Prince, at first with old Jonah leading the horse, then by herself. Soon she was riding so well that her Aunt said she might go outside the gate, and down the road "a piece." Penny wasn't quite sure how far "a piece" might be, but one thing she did want; that was to ride as far as the white house with the white picket fence. She wanted to see the red-headed boy again—and she wanted him to see her too, riding Prince!

Aunt Penelope had told her not to go fast, and she was careful to obey. Slowly she guided the horse along under the elms and maples. But even at that—so much longer are a horse's legs than a small girl's—before she expected it she was there, in front of the rambling white farm house. And —yes, there was the boy!

But he wasn't giving a circus this day. He was standing beside the covered stone well in the side yard, busily turning a handle. He stopped for a moment as Penny came in sight, and glanced at her; then gave the handle another turn, and as the dripping wooden bucket rose, he grasped the rope and pulled it onto the well coping.

Penny rode on past.

She felt terribly disappointed. She had hoped that when she saw the boy again he would be glad to see her too, and say hello; they would become friends, visit each other, and have all sorts of good times. Perhaps he also had a horse and they could take rides together; she was sure he liked to go fishing—and he might let her go with him. She would carry the basket with their lunch in it, and they would picnic beside a stream. Maybe they could give a circus together, too; with Wonderful Willie, of course, and Pouf might learn some tricks—he could if he wanted to, she knew; and she herself would dress up, and dance, and sing. The barn would make a fine place for a circus, and Auntie and Mister Jonah would come to see it—perhaps the boy's Gramp would come too. . . .

But now—he did not even remember her, apparently. Probably she had been just someone to show off to, not to play with. Doubtless he had no use for girls. Still, she had liked him very much. He'd been nice and polite, and, best of all, he seemed to know how to "pretend."

Penny sighed deeply as she rode slowly on, not caring, now, where she was going. She remembered that she had thought it might impress the boy because she was riding Prince, but evidently it hadn't.

Then suddenly it occurred to her that he might have thought *she* was just showing off.

"Well, maybe I was—a little," she admitted. "I did want him to notice—though I didn't feel smarty-proud about it. But perhaps I looked as if I did, just riding by, hardly turning my head. After all, I didn't speak to him either, I was hoping he'd say hello. Why shouldn't I have said it? *Someone* has to say it first. . . . Well, I *will!*"

She turned Prince, heading him back the way she'd come. Her lips were pressed tight together and her heart beat faster. But as she neared the white farmhouse her courage began to melt; she almost wished she would not see the boy at all—

But there he was, sitting on the farmhouse steps with Willie at his feet. He was reading a book, and didn't look up.

"Suppose," thought Penny, "he *doesn't* want to speak to me? Suppose he won't even answer when I say hello?" And the "curled-up-inside feeling" made her quite sure that her voice wouldn't come out at all, no matter how she tried—

"But I'll try," she told herself, remembering her talk with Aunt Penelope. And as Prince, at his gentle pace, was just at the gate in the picket fence and about to pass it, she pulled on the reins. The horse stopped.

"H-hello," said Penny, hardly above a whisper. She made another effort and repeated, loudly, "Hello!"

It seemed quite a long time to Penny before the boy looked up. But at last he did.

"Hello," he said, holding the book tightly, and with a half-awake look in his eyes that Penny understood very well. And because she did, her shyness disappeared.

"Excuse me," she said, "I don't want to interrupt, I know your book must be awfully interesting; but I—I wasn't sure if you remembered me. I came to your circus the other day, you know—and I wanted to tell you I thought it was just simply splendid."

The boy got up and came toward the gate. He still clutched his book, but Penny had called his thoughts out from between its pages.

He said slowly, "Sure I remembered you. But when you just—just rode on by, I—" He shuffled his feet, scraped a long mark in the dusty path with his bare toe, then suddenly looked up at Penny.

She was smiling gravely, and all at once he grinned.

"Say," he said eagerly, "have you ever read this? I'm just at the part where Tom and Becky are in the cave, we're lost—"

He held out the book, and Penny read the title, "The Adventures of Tom Sawyer."

She shook her head. "I haven't read it. But I'd like to—"

At that moment a voice called "Caleb! Ca-*leb!*"

"Gosh, I gotta go," said the boy. "That's Gramp calling—" He looked down at his book wistfully.

"Oh dear—if I hadn't interrupted you'd—maybe you'd have found your way out of the cave by now!" said Penny.

The boy smiled cheerfully. "Oh, I don't mind!" he said. And added, "Say, if I give another circus soon, would you like to come? There won't be any peanuts—I ate what was left—but we can have lemonade. And—and you don't have to pay for it—"

"Oh, I'd love to come!" said Penny. "And, Caleb, couldn't *you* come to our house too? I don't live very far, just down the road. It's the big gray house with the iron railing around it; my Aunt Penelope's house. My name is Penny. Could you come *tomorrow?*"

"Caleb! Caleb, where are you?" came the call again.

"Gosh, excuse me," said Caleb. He started towards the house. Then he turned back and said, "I'd like to—I'll ask Gramp." From the farmhouse steps he waved and called, "Well, g'bye, Penny!"

He disappeared within the house before Penny could reply, but that didn't matter.

"Gedap, Prince!" she said gayly, and the horse started up almost at a canter. Penny rode home feeling very happy.

10. CALEB'S GRAMP

NEXT DAY SHE WAITED, thinking that Caleb would appear.
But he didn't. "Probably he's busy," she said to herself;
and as she was busy too, working and playing, she didn't
worry.

But when another day went by, and then another, she felt
very much disappointed.

That evening she played Lotto so badly (she had meanwhile learned to play it very well) that her Aunt said,
"What's the matter, darling? Do you want to tell me?"

So Penny told her all about Caleb. When she had finished she said, "I guess his Gramp wouldn't let him come
to visit me, Auntie. Because truly I know he would have
—if he could."

Aunt Penelope didn't reply for a while. Slowly she folded
the Lotto board.

Finally she said, "Perhaps his Gramp is shy—like us.
You see, nobody but you—and Jonah—knows *I'm* shy; I've

lived here so long in this big house behind iron railings, not knowing how to make friends with people. But *now—*"

She sat up very straight and her cheeks were a bright pink.

"You were brave today, Penny," she said. "So I will be, too. Tomorrow we will go and call on Caleb and Gramp!"

The next morning, right after their household tasks were done, they set off up the road with Pouf at their heels. Aunt Penelope couldn't walk very fast, and Penny was so eager that her white-stockinged legs kept moving ahead. So she stopped now and then to pick wild-roses from the meadows beside the road.

"Perhaps Gramp will like a bouquet," she said. "I didn't see any flowers at all in their yard."

At last they came to the gate in the picket fence. There was no one in sight. Aunt Penelope opened the gate and walked firmly up the dirt path. Penny and Pouf followed and Aunt Penelope lifted the knocker and rapped it sturdily against the door.

They waited. No one answered, and Aunt Penelope knocked again. Finally they heard steps within the house and the door opened. A tall thin old man with long hair and chin-whiskers stood there. He stared at Aunt Penelope, looking surprised and puzzled.

Aunt Penelope said, very quickly, "Good morning, Mister Peters. I—I hope we're not disturbing you. I'm Miss—"

"Come in, Miss Prichard," said the old man. He opened the door wide. Evidently he knew Aunt Penelope, and obviously he was alarmed. "Is something the matter? Can I do something—?"

Aunt Penelope held out her hand. (It was shaking a little, but Penny thought only she noticed that.) She said, "You can shake hands with me. There's nothing the matter,

except that I haven't known how to be a friendly neighbor
for all these years. But I'd like to be. And your grandson
and my grandniece have started being friends. So—"

Mister Peters took Aunt Penelope's hand; he shook it
gravely.

"Why, I'm right pleased— Come in, come in!" he said,
and backing into the hall, led them into the parlor.

It was a small room, very neat, with ornaments stiffly
arranged on the mantel, and crocheted tidies on the furni-
ture. Aunt Penelope sat down in a horse-hair-covered chair
and Penny took one beside her. ("Where, oh where is
Caleb?" she was wondering.) Just as Mister Peters also was
about to seat himself he started up.

"Jehosaphat!" he exclaimed, and shot out of the parlor.

Aunt Penelope's eyes widened. She sniffed.

"Something's burning. It's *pie!*" she cried, and followed
Mister Peters. Penny ran after them, and into a big, shabby,
untidy kitchen where Mister Peters was yanking open the
over door.

He pulled out a smoking blackened pie.

"Goshdangit all!" he said sadly. Then he turned to Aunt
Penelope. "Excuse me, Ma'am. But it's ruint. And my boy
does like pie. I been tryin' to get the knack of it, but I
don't seem to—"

"Never mind! Just show me where the flour is—and the
shortening—and—"

Aunt Penelope's eyes were sparkling. She began to bustle
around the kitchen, and soon she had found all sorts of in-
gredients and was whipping egg-whites for meringue, rolling out pastry, stirring up cake and a batch of cookies. Penny pared and sliced apples and hulled berries, and Mister
Peters stood watching with an expression of dazed admira-
tion, until Aunt Penelope set him to shelling and chopping
nuts, which he did very clumsily but with a right good will.

"Just to think," said Aunt Penelope, while she worked, "here you've been, just down the road, two hungry men to make goodies for—and I never knew! Mister Peters, how long has this been going on?"

So Mister Peters told her that Caleb had lost his Ma and Pa and had come to live with his Gramp and Granny when he was a "little shaver." The three of them had been very happy together as long as Granny lived.

"Since then—that's 'most a year now—I been doin' for him the best I could. He's a right good lad, and a deal of help to me, too; Gran brought him up good. He chops kindlin', and takes care of the chickens and Flossie and her calf," said Mister Peters. He held out the bowl of nut meats, and inquired anxiously, "Am I doin' these right, ma'am?"

Aunt Penelope brushed the back of one floury hand across her eyes; but she answered brightly, "Yes indeed, you're doing wonderfully. And here are my pies, all ready for the oven."

She popped them in, and began stirring the nut meats into the cake batter.

Just then a screen door slammed, bare feet thudded across the back porch, and Caleb's red head and freckled face appeared in the kitchen doorway. He looked so astonished that Penny burst into a delighted laugh.

"Hello, Caleb!" she cried.

Caleb gulped, but couldn't seem to find voice to reply.

"Speak up, son—where's your manners?" said his Gramp. "These ladies come to pay us a call. Miss Prichard, this here young scalawag is my gran'son, Caleb."

Caleb swallowed again, and managed to say, "Howdy-do, Miss Prichard. H-hullo, Penny."

Penny couldn't help giggling, not at Caleb, but because

"paying a call" had such a parlor company sound; and her Aunt's eyes were twinkling too, as she said, "We *are* funny callers, aren't we? Walking right in and turning your kitchen upside down—cooking you right out of house and home! I wouldn't call *that* exactly manners, but it's great fun!"

Caleb had recovered from his astonishment and grinned back at her. "It smells awful good," he said, wrinkling his freckled snub-nose as he sniffed the fragrant scent of baking.

"Just wait till you *taste* it!" said Penny.

Caleb was gazing thoughtfully at Aunt Penelope, who was now filling cake-tins with a creamy, rich-looking mixture. She had found a gingham apron somewhere and tied it around her; it was much too big for her, and her cheeks were rosy-red from the heat of the stove and there was a dab of flour on the tip of her nose.

"How cute she looks," thought Penny, and wondered if that was what Caleb was thinking too, when he said, slowly, "You—you look kinda like my Gran—except you're littler. Doesn't she, Gramp?"

His Gramp's brown wrinkled face looked slightly embarrassed. But Aunt Penelope was pleased and touched.

"That's a lovely thing to say, Caleb. Thank you!" She smiled at him, and added, "Would you call me Aunt Penelope? I don't feel a bit 'Miss Prichard-y.' And I'm certainly not acting it!" she chuckled.

Penny carefully stemmed the last berry, and asked, "What shall I do next, Auntie?"

Her Aunt said, "Well, my cakes are all ready to go in the oven as soon as my pies come out; I'm afraid there *isn't* much more to do. Suppose you and Caleb take two spoons and these cake bowls out on the back porch, while I clean up in the kitchen—"

So Penny and Caleb settled themselves on the back steps, and slowly scraped off the delicious batter that clung to

the sides of the mixing-bowls, and licked their spoons with relish.

"I think this is almost the nicest part of the cake, don't you?" said Penny.

"Ummmmn," Caleb nodded. "And Aunt Penelope left quite a lot; I think she did it on purpose. Gran used to, too."

They plied their spoons in silence for a moment or so; then Penny said, "I—I thought you were coming over to our house, Caleb. But I suppose you didn't get time? Your Gramp says you take care of the chickens, and—lots of other things."

"Sure, I do, but I got lotsa time—that is, in vacation. Besides the chickens I only got Flossie and her calf, and the kindling, and weeding and picking berries, or peas and beans and tomatoes and such when they come ripe. Gramp does the ploughing and sowing and reaping; and he cooks our vit'ls. Missus O'Brian from down the road a piece does our washing and mending and cleans house once a week. But she's awful cranky; *I'd* rather leave things dirty," said Caleb, scowling. "But Gramp says Gran wouldn't like it " He sighed.

He finished his last bit of batter, and added, "And Gramp said he didn't think your Aunt would like it if I went over to her house. He said she'd lived there all these years, and kept herself to herself—'like her Ma before her,' was what he said. So, he said, he guessed I'd better not go."

Penny thought this over. She understood now, that her Aunt hadn't really wanted to "keep herself to herself"— only she hadn't known how not to. But she couldn't explain it all.

She could only say, "Well, but now you can see—she'd really like you to come?"

Her companion was finishing some thoughts of his own.

He said, "I didn't like that big old *house,* either. It looks like—well, sorta like a house in a cemetery, or a prison, or something. With that high railing all around, and everything so stiff and quiet inside—"

"Oh, but it's not like that!" exclaimed Penny eagerly. Then she remembered how she herself had felt about it at first. She went on, "I mean, inside it's not. Not when you know Aunt Penelope."

They were interrupted by Aunt Penelope herself, who came to the screen door and pushed it open with her shoulder. She had a saucer-sized pie in each hand.

"I made these two little ones so you could eat them now," she said. "And now, I'm running on home, or Jonah will wonder what's become of me and worry his old head off. But you may stay, Penny; and bring Caleb home to dinner. His grandpa says he may come, and he's promised to have supper with us himself, very soon."

When she had gone Penny and Caleb ate their pies. After that they went to see the chickens, which were in a large wire-fenced yard.

"Most folks just let their chickens run," said Caleb, "but my Gran wouldn't; she said they spoiled all her flower-beds and the grass and all, and made everything 'just a dusty mess'. So Gramp keeps 'em like she wanted, only we can't seem to make the flowers grow good, anyhow."

Penny could hardly leave the fluffy golden balls with their round bright eyes and match-stick legs. Caleb got her away at last by saying, "Aw, come on. Let's go see Dobbin and Nellie. And we can ride 'em, too, 'cause they're not working today. They're in the east pasture lot."

The two sturdy farm horses looked very big to Penny; and she hadn't the slightest idea whether she could stay on one of those broad bare backs, nor how to get up on it. There were no stirrups, and there was no saddle, and Mister Jonah wasn't there to help her up, as he always did, onto Prince's back.

But Caleb said, "Look, you get up there," and pointed to a gnarled apple tree with a low hanging branch.

He led Nellie under the branch, where she stood flicking her tail in a patient though bored manner. Penny wasn't used to climbing trees, but she wouldn't have said so for anything. Digging her fingers into the bark and sticking her toes in, skinning both knees, she managed to pull herself up into the spreading crotch, then to wriggle along the branch until she was perched there just over Nellie's back. But—however was she to get on it? And what if Nellie moved away, just at the wrong minute?

"Well, come *on*," said Caleb.

Penny took a long breath and jumped.

To her surprise she landed firmly and squarely on the horse's back. She grasped Nellie's thick mane, just as Caleb, with a whoop and a leap, landed on Dobbin's back.

"Hi-ya!" he shouted. And Dobbin started off at a lumbering gallop, with Nellie following.

Penny twisted her fingers into Nellie's mane and pushed her heels against the horse's flanks. She wasn't sure she could stick on, but she did. And by the time they had wheeled around the pasture twice she had stopped being frightened. The third time around it was almost fun. And at last, when they stopped and Caleb told her just to "hold on and slide off," she found she could do it.

Just then Mister Peters called, to remind them it was almost dinner time and they "mustn't keep Miss Prichard waitin'."

So Caleb hastily scrubbed his face and hands with water in a tin basin on the back porch. Then at a stern nod from his Gramp he darted into the house and reappeared in a clean shirt and another patched but fresh pair of overalls.

Gramp stood at the gate and watched them go off up the road.

"Have a nice visit, son, and mind your manners," he said, with a pleasant smile on his seamed sun-browned face. "And mind you get back in time to fetch Flossie an' her calf back to home!" he added firmly, but rather as an after-thought.

11. TWO IN A TOWER

AT FIRST, CALEB was somewhat overawed by the elaborate
grey mansion behind the tall iron railing. He looked at the
expanse of lawn, that old Jonah fussed over and kept smooth
with such zealous care, as if it were a delicate green velvet
carpet, much too elegant to be stepped on. He even seemed
afraid he might scratch the surface of the neat straight paths,
and he picked his way along them in such a gingerly manner that Penny wanted to laugh. But she didn't, for she
remembered very well that she herself had had much the
same feelings, though she knew by now that the grass was
sturdier than it looked, and nobody cared in the least how
much she ran and frolicked all over it.

As they went through the dim, high-ceilinged hall Caleb
still walked warily, as if he thought it might be impolite to
look around him—though he did steal an interested glance
at the big stag's head. He sat stiffly in his chair, at dinner—
which they ate at the little table on the back porch that
Penny liked so much—"minding his manners" very hard, for

a while. But Aunt Penelope was so friendly that she had put him quite at his ease before the meal was over.

Afterwards Caleb and Penny ran out to explore the barn, which Caleb agreed would be a fine place for a circus, especially when Penny pointed out that a trapeze could be hung from the rafters.

"Don't you think Pouf would learn to do tricks, too?" she asked. "I'm pretty sure he could—if he *wanted* to."

Caleb looked thoughtfully at Pouf, who was sitting, dignified as usual, in the doorway. Willie, who had tried his best to tease the poodle into playing with him, had given up the attempt for the moment; but from the way he was watching the other dog—with his nose on his paws, his tongue peeping out in his usual smile and his bright eyes eager—it was plain that he was still hopeful.

Caleb said, "Oh, I bet Pouf *wants* to do tricks, all right. But I dunno if he could do as good as Willie; Willie's awful smart."

Hearing his name, the little dog jumped up, wagging all over, dashing first to his master, then to Penny. She patted him; then she stooped and held out her hand. Willie immediately sat up on his hand legs and gave her his paw.

Pouf turned his head the other way.

But Penny wasn't noticing him. "Why, look, Willie's shaking hands with me, too!" she exclaimed. She pumped the little paw up and down, saying, "How do you *do*, Willie!"

Willie barked happily in reply—three short barks.

"And he spoke—he answered me!—Caleb, do you think he'd walk for me, if I asked him? May I try?"

"Sure, I guess he would, he likes you. Go ahead, try," said Caleb proudly. "Only you gotta hold your hand up—high."

Penny nodded. She remembered the way Caleb had done it at his circus. She stood up, stretching out her arm and flicking up her wrist. Willie rose on his hind legs at once, and as Penny backed away he followed, taking small careful steps and grinning.

Pouf got up and stalked off.

"Oh, Willie, you *are* wonderful!" cried Penny, hugging him. "Oh, Pouf, I do wish you would—would be a little less haughty!" she said, over her shoulder; then turned to where the poodle had been.

"Why, he's gone! Pouf—where are you?" she called, jumping up.

"You know what? He's jealous!" said Caleb. "I bet he's been jealous, sort of, ever since he watched Willie at the circus! I told you I bet he *wanted* to learn how to do those tricks too, didn't I? Well, and now you've been making a fuss over Willie and not paying any attention to him, and that's just about the last straw."

"Oh dear! Of course that's what's the matter!" Penny felt so sorry that she was near tears. "And I wouldn't have hurt his feelings for anything. You know, Caleb, he comes and jumps on my bed and cuddles up at night, and he goes everywhere with me; but when other people are around he—"

"I know, he acts highty-tighty; some people are like that," Caleb said simply. "Well, come on. We'd better find him."

They hurried out of the barn. Willie, thinking they were all ready for a romp, leapt and yapped around their feet.

Suddenly Caleb stopped, took a piece of rope out of his pocket, fastened one end to Willie's collar and the other to a staple in the barn door. Penny looked on, surprised.

"I guess he better not be along when you make up with Pouf," Caleb explained. "Now, Willie, you stay there, and behave."

The little dog looked crestfallen; he sat abruptly down, his tail curled under him.

"But won't *his* feelings be hurt now?" Penny asked anxiously.

"Oh no. He's always disappointed when he thinks he's going to have a chance to play with me and then he hasn't, or when I go away. But he knows I'll always come back soon, and when I do he forgives me right away and is happier than ever."

"Do you think Pouf will forgive *me?*" queried Penny. "After all, he hasn't known me a long time, like Willie has you. Besides, they seem to have different kinds of dispositions."

"Well, I think he'll get over being mad when you tell him all about it," said Caleb. "Dogs understand a lot more than most people think. But of course you'll have to explain to him."

"What shall I say? I can't tell him I don't like Willie and think he's awfully sweet and smart, because that wouldn't be true—"

"No, of course not," Caleb agreed. "That wouldn't do any good—he wouldn't believe it anyhow. But I guess you'll know what to say to him when we find him."

"But—oh dear, why haven't we found him? Where has he gone?" said Penny.

While they talked they had been hunting, running all over the grounds, peering under bushes and low-spreading tree-branches—behind the barn, in the tool-shed, in every corner. But Pouf was nowhere to be seen.

"Maybe he's gone in the house," suggested Caleb.

So they dashed into the house through the kitchen door, almost upsetting Mister Jonah, who had been scrubbing the floor and was carrying out a pail of soapy water to pour on the roots of the rose bushes.

"Land's sakes," he remarked, as the suds splashed over on the huge carpet-slippers he wore when he worked around the house. Then he grinned. "Injuns?" he said, and leaping into the air with surprising agility he gave a long loud wild war whoop.

At any other time Penny would have been delighted. But right now all she could think of was the little dog, who had run away, his feelings hurt.

"Mister Jonah, have you seen Pouf?" she panted.

The old man sobered as he saw her troubled face. "Pouf? No, Ah ain' seen him, he didn't come in *heah*. Why? What you-all so discombobulated 'bout?"

"Maybe he went to some other door and Auntie let him

in," said Penny. She couldn't take time to explain now, and
dashed off with Caleb after her. They ran through the
pantry, the dining room, the hall and parlor, scrambling
around on the floor to look under tables and chairs and
sofas, behind the long curtains, everywhere.

No Pouf.

They hurried on upstairs. In the upper hall Aunt Penelope came out of her room, some mending in her hands and
a pleased smile on her face.

"Are you playing tag? Or treasure hunting?" she asked.

"We're hunting for Pouf. I—I hurt his feelings and he
went away," said Penny. "Oh, Aunt Penelope, isn't he with
you?"

Aunt Penelope shook her head. No, Pouf wasn't with
her; she hadn't let him in the house; she hadn't seen him at
all. "But the long windows in the parlors are open, and he
might have come in there while I wasn't looking," she said.

"We've searched all over, downstairs," said Penny. "He
isn't there."

Nor was he in her room, or any of the others upstairs,
either on the second or third floor of the big house. They
had made sure of that when Caleb suddenly said, "Maybe
he snuck off up there."

He pointed up toward the attic door, which stood ajar,
and they scurried up the narrow stairway, and called, and
looked behind the trunks and chests and band-boxes, dis-
carded bureaus and sofas. They covered themselves with
dust and cobwebs. They didn't find Pouf.

"But—this is a kinda nice place," said Caleb, plucking a
clinging cobweb from his nose with a grimy hand and leaving a large smut. "Where does that go?"

"That" was a ladder, reaching to the roof, in the very
middle of the attic. There was no door above it; Penny had
no idea where it went.

"I don't know," she said. "Come *on,* Caleb. Pouf isn't here; he isn't in the house at all. Maybe he's run away. Hurry—we've *got to find him!*"

But Caleb still stared up at the ladder.

"Say, there's a trap-door! I bet it leads to the roof, and we can get out there! Gee, if it isn't locked I bet I can push it open!"

"Well, *Pouf* couldn't. So he can't be there. Please, Caleb, let's hurry." Penny tugged at his arm impatiently.

"You know what?" he said. "Listen; if we can get out on the roof we can look all around, awful far. Maybe from up there we can see him, wherever he is!"

Before Penny had time to reply he was up the ladder. When he reached the top he gave a shove, and what seemed to Penny like a long slice of roof flew up so suddenly that Caleb almost lost his balance.

"Gee, it's on counter-weights!" he said. "It's a wonderful trap-door!" He scrambled up and through it and vanished.

Penny waited, gazing upward. She couldn't see the sky through the oblong opening—what *was* up there? And where was Caleb?

"Caleb!" she called. "Where are you?"

After what seemed to Penny like a very long minute his face appeared.

"Say, Penny, come on up here," he said excitedly.

The ladder was steep and narrow. "But if I can climb a tree I guess I can manage it," she thought.

She did. Caleb took her hand and gave her a tug when she reached the top rungs, and then she looked around. She found herself standing in a tiny circular room; she could have touched the low peaked roof-beams with her finger-tips, and the tops of the round windows that studded the walls were below the level of her eyes.

"Oh," she breathed, "it's lovely!"

"It's like a ship—" said Caleb, "and a tower in a fort— and— Gosh—" Words failed him.

They gazed out of one window after another. At one, a nearby tree reached spreading branches, lacy and green. It was strange to be up among the leaves like this.

From another window they could see the barn, which seemed very different when you looked down on the roof, and the weather-vane, and the dove-cote perched on the ridge-pole. "Which isn't *much* littler than the 'house' we're in now," thought Penny, with a cosy feeling.

Then she took another step, and looked out and saw the road going off in the distance somewhere; and beyond, even more distant, the faraway blue hills. She thought, "Now I'm Sister Ann—and the Princess in the Tower—and—"

Caleb was dreaming his own dreams.

"That's the ocean"—he pointed toward the hills—"and we're pirates. No, let's be a whaler. I'm the Captain, you can be the Mate. We'll sail all over the world—I'll steer—" He grasped an imaginary wheel, turning it a bit to the right, then to the left as he peered out over the waves. "And we can get shipwrecked on a coral island, and build huts, and fight savages. My, it would be nice here if it rained and thundered and lightninged, wouldn't it?"

"Yes, beautiful." Penny shivered deliciously as she imagined it. Then as she turned to another window she exclaimed, "Look at those tiny cows! They look like little wooden toy ones, don't they?"

She pointed to a distant meadow, where two white-and-brown specks on match-stick legs were grazing.

"Why, that's the baby-cow—and the big one that scared me—" She bit her lip, for she hadn't meant to blurt that out. She hoped Caleb wouldn't laugh at her.

He didn't, though he smiled as he said, "That's Flossie and her calf! Flossie wouldn't hurt anybody. But she *is* big," he admitted. And added suddenly, "Gosh, we forgot all about Pouf! Can you see him anywhere, Penny? I wish we had a spy-glass."

Thus recalled to sad reality Penny felt conscience-stricken, and when they had scanned everything below them in every direction without a sight of the little dog, she felt worse. Caleb, too, looked worried.

"But maybe he's gone in the house since we hunted for him," the boy said encouragingly.

Penny almost slid down the ladder in her haste to look again for the poodle. Caleb followed. As he closed the trapdoor he looked up longingly at the tiny turret they were leaving. He was hoping very hard that they could come back there some day soon.

But now Penny had no thought other than to find Pouf. And through the house and the grounds they went again, searching and calling. All in vain. No Pouf.

At last they went to the gate and stared up and down the road.

"But he never goes out by himself. And if he has, now, how shall we find him? We don't know which way he may have gone," said Penny miserably.

"Well, we can try both," Caleb said. "I'll go up-along, toward Barlow's Creek. And you go that way, down-along by our house and—"

He stopped, and said in a very quiet tone, "Here he comes."

Penny turned and looked.

There, from around the corner of the high iron railing within which grew a trim box hedge, walked Pouf. His chin was high in the air, his eyes glanced neither to right nor left, he walked in a most proud and indifferent manner. But he was on his way home.

"Oh, Pouf!" cried Penny, and was about to dash toward

him when Caleb said, "Now, don't get excited. He won't like it—he's feeling embarrassed enough already. If I were you, I'd just act sort of natural. He knows you're glad to see him, and later you can tell him—"

Penny realized that Caleb was perfectly right; and all of a sudden she knew, too, just what to do. As Pouf came up to them, and was about to pass and enter the big gate, she said pleasantly, "How-do-you-do, Pouf? Did you have a nice walk?" And she held out her hand.

Pouf paused. It seemed for a moment as if he were of two minds. Then he sat down, solemnly, lifted his paw and placed it in Penny's outstretched palm. He barked, three times.

Penny shook his paw up and down. Then—she couldn't help it—she sat right down beside the little dog and hugged him.

"Oh, Pouf, I love you better than any dog in all the world," she said softly. And Pouf put out his slender pink tongue, and swiped it delicately, just once, across her chin. Which left one clean spot on her face; but Penny didn't know that.

"Well," said Caleb, "I guess now we'd better go and untie Willie. You know what, I bet? I bet they're going to be good friends, Willie and Pouf."

12. POSIES FOR MRS. O'BRIAN

CALEB WAS RIGHT; in a few days the two dogs were the best of friends. They had wonderful times chasing each other or a ball or a stick; rolling over and over, growling and barking in pretend fights, dashing off together at some sound or secret signal that only they had heard. Or just snoozing side by side in the warm sun, or, on rainy days, curled up in their favorite indoor spots at the farmhouse or The Elms. If Pouf now and then reverted to his highty-tighty manner, or was somewhat bossy, good-natured Willie didn't hold it against him. And when Pouf didn't see Willie for a while it was quite evident that he missed his new friend from the restless way in which he would go to the gate and look up and down the road, several times a day.

Not many days passed, however, when the two little dogs didn't see one another, because Penny and Caleb now spent most of their time together.

It got to be a kind of standing rule for Caleb and Gramp and Penny and her Aunt to have supper together twice a week. On Saturdays, at The Elms; after which they would all play Parchesi; on Wednesdays, at the farmhouse, where Gramp and Aunt Penelope would sit on the porch and rock and talk while Caleb and Penny and Willie and Pouf played hide and seek around the barn and among the lilac bushes.

On the Wednesdays, Aunt Penelope cooked supper. And before that, she always made up a batch of goodies to last "their two hungry men-folk" through the week. Sometimes Penny helped. Sometimes she and Caleb picked vegetables, most of which Gramp took to market, but Aunt Penelope "put up" a lot too, in the thick glass jars or big stone crocks that Gran had once used.

"There'll be plenty now, against the Winter," she said contentedly.

"But I won't be here then," said Penny wistfully. Then she quickly put that thought out of her mind, which wasn't hard, because there were always so many things to do.

Nellie and Dobbin soon became her friends. When they saw her coming they always pricked their ears and whinnied softly.

"Listen—they know my name!" she told Caleb, only half jokingly. "They're saying 'Pe-eh-eh-eh-neeeee'—just as plain!" And she laughed and stroked the soft noses as they nuzzled her to find the sugar or apples she often brought them in her pinafore pocket. Afterwards, she and Caleb would get on the broad backs, and have a fine gallop.

There was another kind of pleasure in riding the black iron deer, which of course never went anywhere at all; but perhaps for that very reason Penny and Caleb found, when they climbed on his hard slippery back, that they could speed away to any place in the wide world they wanted to go.

Then there were times when they didn't feel like pretending at all; when it was blissful simply to race barefooted over the grass, or to practice jumping from the hayloft. And Penny learned to play Mumblety Peg, and even to shoot marbles.

Of course, there was work to do, too; especially for Caleb, because Gramp depended on him, even if he was only nine years old. But Penny often helped him. It was fun to feed the chickens, to gather the big warm eggs, to fetch Flossie and her adorable calf home, to watch Caleb milk her. Once Penny begged to try herself. But Flossie, at the first touch of unfamiliar hands, upset the half full bucket.

"I guess I'd better wait till next Summer before I try again. By that time she'll be more used to me." said Penny, wiping milk from her face.

"Well, maybe it isn't right work for a girl anyway," said Caleb. "Nor lugging wood and water nor chopping kindling nor cleaning chicken houses. When I was too little to be much use Gramp did all those things himself, he wouldn't ever let Gran."

So Penny too was barred from helping with those chores —which to tell the truth she didn't think she'd enjoy very much.

"But there *are* some useful things I can do *better* than Caleb," she decided, and while he was busy she would tie Gran's big gingham apron around her neck, and sweep and dust. She felt very grown-up and house-wifey bustling around with her broom and duster, and proud of the tidy rooms when she had finished with them.

But Caleb was impatient if she were still "fussing 'round" (as he called it) when he was through with his special chores. He admitted, however, that it gave Mrs. O'Brian less to do, so she "wasn't 'round so much, clucking and clattering," which he considered a blessing.

Penny couldn't help agreeing with him about that. Mrs. O'Brian was a bedraggled tired looking woman who de-

scribed her various aches and pains and grievances in de-
tail, and with groans, as she washed the windows or scrubbed the floor or beat the rugs—which was the only thing
she did with any appearance of satisfaction.

Penny was sorry for her. "But," as she said to Aunt
Penelope, "she *isn't* cheerful company. Somehow, she always makes me feel bad because I can't help feeling good;
you know, as if it's selfish of me not to have all those 'ails',
as she calls them, when she has to have them. Do you think
it is, Auntie?"

Penny had been really troubled about this, as her Aunt
understood. She put down her knitting. She took some time
to reply, and when she did it was with a question.

"It wouldn't help Mrs. O'Brian's ailments for you to
have them too, would it?"

"N-o. No, I know that, of course," answered Penny.
"Only—sometimes she makes it seem as if even the sun
wasn't shining. So I just run off the minute she begins
telling me her troubles, or even when I see her coming.
And then I feel worse."

"Well, darling," said Aunt Penelope, "I guess, then, that
you'd best listen to Mrs. O'Brian's troubles once in a while.
Maybe just someone listening will make her feel better.
And by listening, you might think of some other ways too
to make her feel happier; and then *you'd* feel better."

Penny thought this over. She couldn't see any way in
which she could cure Mrs. O'Brian's neuralgia and sciatica
and bronchitis and dyspepsia, which their possessor said
"the doctors had already given up." And once, when Mrs.
O'Brian had been groaning about her "terrible knee,"
Penny had offered to scrub the kitchen floor instead; but
Mrs. O'Brian had retorted very crossly.

"Thin what?" she snapped. "Could I be takin' money
for scrubbin' I'm not afther doin'? An' without the bit o'

money I earn scrubbin' an' washin', how'll I be after keepin
food in me mouth and a roof over me head? Tell me that!"

Penny couldn't tell her that, nor could she find answers
to the many other angry questions Mrs. O'Brian asked (to
which, as a matter of fact, she didn't seem to expect answers,
for she just went on from one to another without pause.)
But as Penny thought this all over now she suddenly remembered something—

"Auntie, do you know the only thing I've ever heard
Mrs. O'Brian say she liked? It was a pansy, the only one
left that Caleb's Gran had planted, near the front steps.
Well, she didn't even really *say* she liked it, but I saw her
looking at it. And as she picked up the basket of wash
and went off I heard her muttering to herself, 'And even
if I cud buy posy-seeds and had time to 'tend 'em, the pig'd
be after ruinin' 'em.' " Penny clasped her hands, her eyes
were eager as she went on, "May I take her a bunch of
flowers? Very special ones, I mean—from our Secret Garden!"

"That's a wonderful idea!" said Aunt Penelope.

So the very next day they cut a beautiful bouquet of the
loveliest, most golden and purple pansies they could find
in the Secret Garden, and mingled yellow-pink rosebuds
with them. Penny said, "I think she'd like little, silk-and-
velvety flowers most—I don't know why. But maybe if she
is pleased with these, we'll try peonies and gladiola and
stock and phlox and prince's feather and our big red roses
on her too—shall we, Auntie?"

Her Aunt agreed, and Penny went off down the road. It
wasn't Mrs. O'Brian's cleaning day at the farm-house, so
she was going to take her gift to Mrs. O'Brian's own home,
which was down a lane just past the farm. She hoped Mrs.
O'Brian would be in.

She hoped, even more fervently yet with more and more

qualms, that Mrs. O'Brian wouldn't be very annoyed.

"Suppose she feels like she did when I wanted to scrub the floor?" she thought. And when she reached Caleb's house, and he ki-yied to her from the chicken-yard, she almost gave up her whole idea.

"I could just take these in and put them in the jug on the kitchen table," she thought. But she didn't.

"I'm on an errand, I'll be back soon!" she called to Caleb, and hurried past, holding the bouquet so he couldn't see it. (She didn't want to explain about it later.)

She soon came to the lane which led to Mrs. O'Brian's house—or so she had heard; she had never been there. It was hardly a lane at all—more like a dusty weed-grown path, with now and then a wheel-rut showing. She couldn't see Mrs. O'Brian's house, or any house at all.

But she went on, and suddenly the lane turned, and there, in a hollow beyond a big clump of sumach, was a small shabby cottage. It really looked more like a shed, with its flat sagging roof that had a piece of stove-pipe sticking out of it, and only two windows, one of which was broken. A few scraggly chickens wandered around, picking at the bare dusty earth in a discouraged way. But Penny was quite sure it was Mrs. O'Brian's home, partly because the clothes-lines were full of flapping clothes, and partly because there was the pig Mrs. O'Brian had mentioned, and partly because it looked like Mrs. O'Brian.

So she walked up to the door and knocked. A voice inside shrilled, "Who's there?"

Heavy footsteps thumped across the floor, the door was yanked open. Mrs. O'Brian stood there.

Penny said timidly, "Good morning."

Mrs. O'Brian didn't return the greeting. She wiped her soapy arms on her wet apron. She looked hot and tired and unhappy and cross as usual.

"Well? And what is it?" she said.

Penny was now perfectly sure it had been a mistake to come. But here she was. What could she do?

Stiffly she stuck out her hand with the flowers in it.

"We—we thought you might like these flowers," she said in a weak voice, and tried to smile.

Probably the smile was not much of a success; anyway Mrs. O'Brian didn't smile back. Nor did she take the flowers.

Staring at them, then at Penny, she said, "Who is 'we'?"

"My—my Aunt Penelope and—and me," said Penny.

"And why would I be afther wantin' yure flowers?" said Mrs. O'Brian.

"We—we like flowers. We just thought you would like them, too—"

"Well, I don't. You kin kape thim," said Mrs. O'Brian.

At first tears came to Penny's eyes; but suddenly the tears turned to rage, and spilled over. Her voice was low, but it shook as she said, "No, I won't keep them. I brought them for you. But if you don't want them, maybe your pig will."

She threw the pansies and roses toward the pig, who was scratching himself against a rain barrel, and turned and walked off. She wanted to run, but she wouldn't let herself —at least, until she was past the clump of sumach and well away from Mrs. O'Brian's house.

Then she ran as fast as she could, straight home. She was thankful that Caleb wasn't in sight when she passed his house, because she didn't want to stop, she didn't want to talk to him then—or to anyone. When she reached The Elms she slipped hastily upstairs to her own room and flung herself on the bed, face downward, squeezing her eyelids tight.

But that didn't shut out the picture of herself holding out the flowers, and of Mrs. O'Brian's angry offended face.

And then, she had behaved like a crybaby, losing her temper and flinging down the flowers! The poor unwanted pansies and rosebuds, that had been so gay and smiling-looking. She could still see them lying where they'd fallen, beside a rusty tin can at the edge of a soapy, muddy puddle.

"I'll never speak to that mean old woman again. I hate her. I'll never be nice to *anyone* ever again—" Penny clenched her fists and her anger was like a hard, burning stone in her chest.

She lay there for a long while, going over and over the ugly, humiliating scene; telling herself miserably that she couldn't go to Caleb's house any more either, because Mrs. O'Brian might be there and she couldn't bear ever to see her again; thinking resentfully of Aunt Penelope too—after all, it was she who had suggested trying to make that cross old woman happy.

"Happy! I don't believe anything could make her happy, I believe she *likes* all her 'ails'!" said Penny aloud, bitterly.

Finally all these unpleasant thoughts and feelings became blurry, and she fell into an uncomfortable restless doze, through which, at last, penetrated a soft rap-rap-rapping, and Aunt Penelope's voice, "Penny, Penny! May I come in, dear?"

"Yes," answered Penny shortly.

The door opened, and her Aunt came in. The moment she saw Penny's face she put her arms around the little girl. "Why, darling! What's happened?"

And Penny, who had felt that she couldn't tell anyone—not anyone, ever—what had happened, suddenly clung to her Aunt and burst out with the whole story.

Aunt Penelope listened quietly. When Penny had told it all her Aunt didn't say anything at once.

Then she sighed. "Well, I'm afraid we just made a mistake, darling. But we certainly didn't intend to hurt Mrs. O'Brian's feelings. I'm sorry yours got hurt. Let's have dinner now. When we're through Jonah would like you to help him in his vegetable patch."

Penny washed her face and went down to dinner. Afterwards, as she pulled the tough little weed sprouts from the rich earth between the rows of radishes and onions she felt much better. And just as she'd finished her last row Caleb appeared.

"Where'd you go this morning?" he asked. "I thought you were coming over to my house."

Penny didn't feel like explaining. "Come on, let's play stage-coach!" she said.

They played stage-coach, which was a pretend game Caleb had invented. They got into the antiquated covered carriage in the barn, and drove it furiously across the prairies pursued by highwaymen or Indians. Sometimes, ambushed, they jumped out, hiding behind hummocks and mesquite bushes as they bang-banged away with their trusty six-shooters. When the enemy bit the dust they leapt back and galloped on again. It was a noisy, almost too scary game which Penny didn't usually like as much as Caleb did, but today she felt like playing it more than anything else.

And when it was time for Caleb to go home he said, "Gee,

you sure aimed good today, Penny. You musta shot 'most as many of those mail-robbers as I did! Say, would you like to come fishing to the Creek with me tomorrow?"

This was one of the things Penny had dreamed of. And she knew that several times Caleb had gone off with his fishing rod over his shoulder and Willie at his heels. But they had not before asked her to go with them.

"Yes, we'd like to go," she replied, trying not to sound too excited.

"Well, then, you come by 'bout nine o'clock. Gramp says I can stay all day, and take some sandwiches along—"

"Let me bring them!" exclaimed Penny.

The next morning she and Pouf set out. Penny carried a basket with not only sandwiches in it but hard-boiled eggs, and salt, and pickles and two big pieces of orange layer cake, all covered neatly with a large red napkin. Caleb and Willie were waiting for her, at the farm-house gate.

Penny felt very happy—until they turned into the lane that led to Mrs. O'Brian's house. Then she stopped short.

"Is—is the Creek down *there?*" she faltered.

"Yep," said Caleb. "Gee—lookit that blacksnake! He's a whopper!"

One of the many things that Penny had learned during the last few weeks was that blacksnakes wouldn't hurt her. But she stood there stock-still in the middle of the rutty path, and Caleb turned to see what was the matter.

"Say, you're not scared of him, are you?" he asked.

"No," said Penny.

"Well, come on, then," said Caleb.

Penny followed him. She thought, "I'll just walk by. I hope that horrid old Mrs. O'Brian isn't around, but if she is, I won't pay any attention anyway."

She meant to keep her eyes straight ahead; but as they passed the shanty she couldn't help glancing at it.

And there on the rickety front stoop, in a small blue pitcher, was the nosegay of pansies and rosebuds she had tossed on the ground. The pig hadn't got them, after all! Someone *had* wanted them.

Just then Mrs. O'Brian appeared around the corner of the house. Her thin mouth was full of clothespins, which she took out to remark, "Goin' fishin', are ye? Well, I kin tell ye right now ye won't ketch nothin' but yure death o' colds. Unless ye stumble in an' drownd yuresilfs, like me sister Mamie's Aloysius—"

Caleb grabbed Penny's arm and hurried her along, but they could hear Mrs. O'Brian's dire warnings following them as long as they were in sight. When they were out of ear-shot Caleb said, "She gives me a pain."

Penny was smiling.

"What's the joke?" asked Caleb.

"Oh, I just feel good. It's such a beautiful day—and it's the first time I've ever gone fishing," said Penny.

All the rest of the lovely day—while they fished, and waded, and threw sticks for the dogs to retrieve from the creek, and ate their lunch, and discovered a woodchuck hole, and filled the empty lunch-basket with wild black-berries—all day, every now and then, Penny remembered. She had seen not only the flowers in the little cracked pitcher; besides, there had been a rosebud and **a pansy** pinned at the neck of Mrs. O'Brian's dress.

13. SUGAR FOR WILLIE

PENNY CAUGHT ONE FISH and Caleb caught four.

"That makes them divide just right," he said, as they trudged homeward. "One for you, one for Aunt Penelope, one for Mister Jonah, one for Gramp and one for me."

Aunt Penelope cooked their share for supper. She said hers was delicious.

"Mighty nice—I sho' enjoyed mine," said Mister Jonah, coming from the kitchen with the dessert. "Yassir, ain't nothin' tastes better'n frash ketched feesh!"

Penny thought so too.

While they ate she told Aunt Penelope all about the wonderful day. She kept the story of what had really happened to the pansies and rosebuds till the very end.

Aunt Penelope was as pleased about it as she was.

"And are you going to try the peonies and gladiola on her next?" she asked, her eyes twinkling.

"We-ell, maybe," said Penny. "But not till I'm sure she'll

be politer if I do. I certainly do *not* feel like being a meeky-cheek goody-good."

As it happened Mrs. O'Brian's cleaning day at the farm house didn't come around for almost a week; Penny had forgotten all about it when, one morning, she and her Aunt picked an armful of bright red roses and bridal wreath for the farmhouse. Penny, with Pouf trotting beside her, carried it over, and as she got to the kitchen door she saw Mrs. O'Brian down on her hands and knees surrounded by a lake of soapy water.

The woman heard her at the door and groaned, without looking up, "Arrah, hivins above. Must ye be comin' in here and dirtyin' up me flure I'm just afther gettin' clane? Filthy it was; and me with me back near splittin' in two and the rheumatiz rackin' me jints night afther night till I cudn't slape a wink—"

Then she glanced up. She saw the flowers in Penny's arms. She didn't say anything—but Penny saw how she looked at them.

Penny gulped. Suddenly she knew she was going to swallow her pride and risk another rebuff. Also she was going to tell a sort of fib.

"These are for you," she said. "Aren't they p-pretty?" she held out her bouquet.

Mrs. O'Brian stared. Then she hitched herself slowly up to her feet and reached out her red scrawny hands and took the flowers.

"We used to have gilliflowers and periwinkle and Michaelmas daisies bloomin' in the yard, in the Ould Country. And red red roses climbin' all over the chimbly," she muttered. And added grudgingly, "Well, thank ye kindly."

Penny, followed by Pouf, flew off to look for Caleb. She found him in the orchard gathering cherries.

"Hi! Come on up!" he called.

"No, you come down!" Penny called back. "I've got something to show you!" She made her voice sound very mysterious.

Caleb scrambled down.

Penny had her hand in her pinafore pocket and he asked, interestedly, "What is it? Treasure?"

(Because they did find all sorts of treasure—pebbles, round and pinky-white like pearls, jewel-like bits of colored glass, pieces of stone flecked with gold, and many other things.)

Now, without answering, Penny took her hand slowly out of her pocket and held it out. On it lay a lump of sugar.

"Well, for goodness sake, what's so wonderful about that!" exclaimed Caleb, disgusted.

She giggled at his expression, then made her own mysterious again.

"Wait," she said, in a solemn whisper.

She called, "Pouf! Come here please, Pouf."

Pouf obeyed.

Slowly, carefully, Penny placed the lump of sugar on his pointed nose.

"You won't eat it, will you Pouf, until I say you may?" She shook her head.

Pouf moved his head, carefully, from side to side. The sugar almost toppled, but it didn't—quite.

"Well, it's for you, you may eat it!" said Penny in a loud cheery voice, and the poodle tossed the tid-bit up, then caught it in his mouth.

"Good, isn't it?" said Penny, with the appropriate gesture; and Pouf, crunching, nodded agreement.

Caleb had watched fascinated. So had Willie. In fact, Willie had been almost spell-bound. Now as he watched the sugar disappear he sat down abruptly, drooling.

"Gosh," Caleb said. "Gosh." Then he added, "You got any more sugar, Penny?"

"Yes," she answered, "I brought some for Dobbin and Nellie."

"Will you lend 'em to me, for Willie?"

In her excitement over Pouf's new accomplishment Penny had forgotten poor little Willie. Now as she noticed his wistful waiting expression she was sorry.

"Of course. I'll get more for the horses," she said, and gave Caleb the sugar.

"Here, Willie!" he said. "Now, don't you eat it until I tell you to!" He shook his head, and kept shaking it as he held the sugar out and started to place it on the little dog's nose.

But Willie hadn't got the idea. Snap-gllup-scrunch, and the sugar was gone. The same thing happened with the next piece. Willie wagged and smiled all over. But his master was disgusted.

"Haven't you any sense? Why don't you mind what I say?" he demanded.

Just then Penny's eye fell on Pouf, who had walked away with a very superior expression, and was now looking on in his most top-lofty manner.

"Well, *you* needn't be so smarty-proud, it took five lumps before you understood what I meant!" she said. "Come on, Caleb, let's go over to Auntie's and get more for Willie to learn with."

"All right," said Caleb. Then he remembered that he'd promised Gramp to take a basket of cherries to Aunt Penelope and the basket was only half full. So Penny scrambled up into the tree (she was very good at climbing by this time) and helped, and the big basket was soon brimming, and they hurried off with it to The Elms.

It took a great deal of coaxing and scolding, and *twelve* lumps of sugar before Willie learned what was expected of him, at which his master was somewhat disgruntled.

"Well," said Aunt Penelope, who had come out on the porch to watch, "Willie's that much sugar ahead. Maybe he had that all figured out! As for Pouf, he would never have learned what fun it is to be sociable and entertaining except for Willie."

So Caleb and Willie went home content—and with a plateful of cherry tarts.

That evening after supper Penny and her Aunt were sitting on the porch watching the fireflies. The night was warm and velvety; the katy-dids-and-didn'ts were arguing; somewhere a whippoorwill called. The frogs croaked and groaned as usual. They reminded Penny of Mrs. O'Brian, and she remembered that she hadn't said "You're welcome" in reply to her "Thank you kindly." But it didn't seem to matter. What mattered was that Mrs. O'Brian had really liked the flowers, after all.

As she said to Aunt Penelope, with a deep happy sigh, "*Everything's* turned out so beauteously." This was a very special word of Penny's.

14. TREASURE TROVE

THERE WERE HOT lazy days when everything seemed to be half dreaming in a quivering sweet-smelling haze, and the shadows of the willows were cool over the Creek, where Caleb taught Penny to swim--with Jonah watching from the bank, while she learned. There were clear breezy days, when it was wonderful to ride horseback with her hair streaming out behind her, or to run wildly over the grass or through the meadows, shouting for pure joy and doing handsprings, another new accomplishment.

The stormy days, and even the time when a cold drizzly rain never stopped falling for a whole week, were lovely too. For then Caleb and she had all sorts of other things to do. They gave circuses in the barn, and played hide-and-seek through the big grey mansion that had so many interesting nooks, upstairs and downstairs, to hunt through.

Including the attic. Aunt Penelope didn't mind how much they rummaged. In one of the old horsehair trunks Caleb found a tattered coat and cap that had belonged to

Great-great-granduncle Tom who had been a drummer boy in the Revolutionary War. After that Caleb never wanted to dress up in anything else. Penny liked to be Great-Grandmother Marie Ann Penelope Elizabeth, and she also liked to be a Spanish senorita with a lace scarf and a tall comb, or a gypsy draped in a crimson shawl and a purple kerchief around her head. The attic was lovely.

But best of all, of course, was the turret room. The Castle Tower.

There, when the wind blew and the rain lashed the windows, they were in a ship at sea. On a dull dreary day they might be prisoners, shivering and hungry, planning how to escape. When the sun shone they could be birds or squirrels high among the trees. Or they were themselves, and talked together, or read their favorite books while they nibbled cookies and munched apples.

It was in the Castle Tower, under a loose board in the floor, that they hid their Treasure Trove. In a shiny metal box that her aunt had given Penny were their pearls, and jewels, and nuggets; an exquisite milky-blue marble, a lovely bronze feather, and a tiny shoe that Penny had found. It was green, and hardly more than an inch long—it could have been lost by an elf. It was Penny's favorite treasure.

Caleb had contributed a flat piece of rock on which was imprinted, in delicate outline, the skeleton of a frog; a rusty bullet; and a sharp pointed stone he was sure was an Indian arrowhead. This he loved best of all.

One day when they were gloating over these precious things Caleb said, "When you go away, Penny, how'll we divide them all?"

When he said this, the Treasure suddenly lost most of its enchantment for Penny. She loved to look at the magical things—especially the elf's shoe—but even that would lose much of its charm if it were not a Hidden Treasure.

She said slowly, "I thought we were going to leave them here forever. We'll always know they are here, and we can come back and look at them. You can, any time you want to, even after I go away. And I'm coming back next Summer, you know. And years and years and years afterwards when we're both grown-up and old we can still come back and find it again."

"Well, but *forever*—?" said Caleb.

He picked up the Indian arrowhead and looked at it a long time.

"All right!" he said. "And listen: we got to make a Solemn Pact about it!"

"Oh yes!" cried Penny, excitedly. "And we must write it down! Wait—"

She hurried downstairs, to return with a piece of her notepaper (which otherwise she used only for letters home.)

"Here, you write it," she said, handing Caleb the paper and her small pencil.

He licked the pencil, pondered, then wrote:

"East Riverbridge, July 23, 1904. This is a Solum Pact. We do solumly promise and swear. cross our hearts, that this is our Treasure. And we will leave it Here forever and ever."

Then he and Penny clasped hands and repeated the words; after which they signed their names.

"Wait!" said Caleb, "we got to have a warning too."

Beneath their names he printed:

"P.S. BEWARE. Anybody Else that opens this Treasure Box *BEWARE!!!*"

And underneath that he drew a picture of a skull and crossbones and a dagger with drops dripping from it.

Penny clasped her hands.

"And Caleb!" she exclaimed, "we must always say some Secret Magic Words, *always,* before the Box will open!"

"All right! Let's say—"

He invented three wonderful Magic Words—which no one else but they must ever know. Penny repeated them in a solemn whisper.

Then they opened the Box and laid the paper with their Solemn Pact inside and closed the lid.

"You know what?" said Caleb. "I bet, if anyone even tried to open that Box and didn't say the Words—I bet it wouldn't open!" Then he added, slowly, "But what if *we* forget them?"

"We won't ever forget," said Penny.

15. THE MOST BEAUTEOUS THING

So THE SUMMER PASSED. The ladyslippers and buttercups and daisies left the fields, and there was Queen Anne's Lace. Wild roses waved their petals, then tossed them to the breeze. Tawny tiger-lilies came to take their place, and the gleaming plumes of golden-rod. The sumach turned slowly crimson.

September came; soon school would open; and before that Penny must be going home. Nearer and nearer approached the day. And then it arrived.

It was a bright still day. Penny woke very early in the morning. She was so excited that she got her plaid "traveling dress" buttoned up wrong and had to do it all over again. And then there were the last-minute things—her comb and brush and her night-gown to go in her valise, which she and Aunt Penelope had packed the night before. It was crammed full; besides what she had brought in it were a wooden doll that Gramp had whittled, Caleb's tambourine that he had given her, a penny-bank from Mister

Jonah, a handkerchief from Mrs. O'Brian, a tam-o'shanter knitted by Aunt Penelope, and the shawl and muffler she herself had crocheted for her mother and father. But finally the bag was squeezed shut and fastened by Mister Jonah.

Then it was time for breakfast, though Penny could hardly sit still long enough to eat. As soon as she had finished she put on her jacket and sailor hat. But she had one more thing to do.

Upstairs she ran—up to the Castle Tower. She lifted the loose board, and said the Magic Words, and opened the Treasure Box for one last look.

"Goodbye—until next Summer!" she whispered.

She closed the Box and hid it again.

Then she flew downstairs. Prince and the carriage were already waiting beside the front porch, with Aunt Penelope and Pouf in the back seat.

Aunt Penelope was holding Penny's lunch box, and the brimming satchel was at her feet. Penny jumped in to sit between her and Pouf. Jonah climbed to his seat, gathered up the reins and clucked to Prince. They started off.

Suddenly Penny remembered that she had forgotten—

"Rosmyrelda!" she cried. "Wait—Mister Jonah, please stop!"

The old man chuckled.

"H'yere she am!" he said, and picked Rosmyrelda up from beside him and handed her to Penny.

Penny settled back, feeling a little ashamed of forgetting her old friend. But she hadn't much time to think of that, because Caleb and Gramp were to meet them at the Depot, to say goodbye, and she was already worrying that they might be late.

Sure enough, they were not there when the carriage drew up at the station.

"Oh dear!" cried Penny. "Suppose they don't get here?"

"There's plenty of time, the·train isn't due for almost half an hour," said Aunt Penelope, showing Penny her watch. "Don't worry."

But Penny couldn't help worrying. She kept asking to see the time; and the hands kept creeping around—and still no Gramp—no Caleb.

Finally, off in the distance, the train whistled.

"What shall I do?" said Penny. "I *can't* go without saying goodbye—"

But just then, around a corner galloped Nellie and Dobbin with the farm wagon bumping behind them. Gramp on the front seat was shouting "Gedap!" and Caleb, beside him, hung on to Willie who was barking shrilly. In back, holding on to a hat which was much too small for her with a dilapidated pink rose that was much too big for it, was Mrs. O'Brian.

As they lumbered up Gramp yanked the reins and yelled "Whoa!" He and Mrs. O'Brian clambered out of the wagon as fast as they could. Caleb had already jumped down and dashed toward Penny.

"Willie made us late!" he said, breathlessly. "He ran away—and we didn't want to go without him—so I hunted and hunted! I guess he'd gone to look for Pouf—I found him 'way up the road near Pouf's house—"

"Anyway you got here! Oh, I'm so glad!" said Penny.

Up steamed the train, clanging and clattering as the wheels ground and stopped. There was time only for Penny to hug Aunt Penelope and to call "Goodbye—goodbye till next Summer!"

Then the conductor shouted "A-all aboard!" and swung her up the steps.

Quickly she ran to a window and pressed her face close to the pane.

There they all were, looking up at her from the platform;
Pouf standing on his hind legs, Aunt Penelope holding
his paw and smiling; Willie, grinning and wagging all over,
in Caleb's arms; Gramp waving his gnarled hand and Mister Jonah his shabby high hat and Mrs. O'Brian the end of
her shawl. Penny waved back, and threw kisses, as the train
began to move. As it went faster she pressed closer to the
window, looking back as long as she could at her friends.
And then—they were gone.

She settled back, holding Rosmyrelda tight, as the conductor put her satchel and lunch-box and umbrella on the
seat beside her.

"So you're going all the way to New York," he said kindly,
punching the ticket she handed him and slipping it into
the band around her sailor hat.

Yes, she was going to New York—going home! To Mother
and Father, and Beppo the hurdy-gurdy man and his little
monkey, and Emma and Alice, and the gay city streets. How
wonderful it would be to see them again—and what a lot
she would have to tell everybody!

She had learned so many new things. How to ride Prince
and swim and fish, and crochet, and weed and feed chickens
and gather eggs. And not to be afraid of cows and blacksnakes and hop-toads and wasps and bees. And she knew
the names and ways of all sorts of flowers and vegetables
and birds and insects. And so many stories about the people
in the Album. And new games and pretends. And best of
all, her new friends—Aunt Penelope and Pouf and Caleb
and Willie and Gramp and Mister Jonah and Prince and
Nellie and Dobbin and Mrs. O'Brian. . . .

Suddenly she couldn't *bear* to leave them all. Next Summer—next summer was a long, long time away. . . . Yet, oh,
she longed for her Father and Mother and her home . . .

It was too many mixed up feelings, sad and happy, to

feel all at once. Tears came into Penny's eyes, brimmed and ran down her cheeks. She turned her face to the window and fumbled for her handkerchief.

Then a voice said, "Would you like to play dominoes, little girl? I have some in my bag. Please don't cry."

Penny stiffened.

"I do not want to play dominoes!" she thought. But she glanced across the aisle. A thin, middle-aged woman was smiling at her rather timidly.

Suddenly Penny thought of the old gentleman who had tried to be kind to her when she was setting out on her journey—and was already homesick even if she hadn't quite realized it. And she had a sharp painful memory of herself holding out the pansies and roses to Mrs. O'Brian—and Mrs. O'Brian refusing them. She remembered how she had tried to run away because she and Aunt Penelope had been shy with each other. And she remembered their Secret Pact.

"I must never forget it. It is even more important than the Magic Words that open the Treasure Box," she thought.

She took out her handkerchief and wiped her eyes frankly.

"Thank you, I'd like very much to play dominoes," she said, smiling at the woman across the aisle.

The woman's face lighted up, so that it looked, all at once, quite pretty.

"I guess," said Penny to herself, "the most beauteous thing in the whole world is to *be friendly*."